# TROUBLE AT TAOS

Seth Tobin rescued Ruth Simms from Crow attack, thinking that when they reached Fort Union she would be safe living with her Uncle. But as Seth heads for the Rockies, the trader Almedo and the notorious bandit leader Espinosa lust after Ruth. Soon the body count rises as the sound of guns reverberates through the mountains. Can Seth, and the wily old mountain man Dick McGhee, save Ruth from an awful fate — and reap some gold by way of reward . . . ?

JACKSON DAVIS

# TROUBLE AT TAOS

*Complete and Unabridged*

## LINFORD
*Leicester*

First published in Great Britain in 2007 by
Robert Hale Limited
London

First Linford Edition
published 2008
by arrangement with
Robert Hale Limited
London

British Library CIP Data

Davis, Jackson, *1937 –*
    Trouble at Taos.—Large print ed.—
Linford western library
1. Western stories
2. Large type books
I. Title
823.9'14 [F]

ISBN 978–1–84782–165–2

Published by
F. A. Thorpe (Publishing)
Anstey, Leicestershire

Set by Words & Graphics Ltd.
Anstey, Leicestershire
Printed and bound in Great Britain by
T. J. International Ltd., Padstow, Cornwall

This book is printed on acid-free paper

# 1

'Ai-yai-yee!' The Mexican chieftain, Espinosa, at the head of his band of twenty *viciosos*, galloped across the plateau of chapparal and spotted the town of Taos appearing through the heat-haze. 'There it is!'

He hauled in his wild-eyed mustang on a rise looking down at the ancient Spanish town which now, in the mid 1850s, was expanding with more timber and clapboard establishments built by an influx of American settlers.

'First I kill the *Americano* and we take Teresa with us,' he yelled. 'Then you can loot the town. You know what we need.'

For the most feared bandit in Colorado territory Espinosa was a re-markably handsome man. He removed his wide-brimmed sombrero to wipe sweat from his brow beneath a head of thick black curls. He flashed a smile in a countenance the colour of mahogany, checked his revolver and said, 'Don't forget, the gambler is mine.'

It was a matter of family honour. News had reached him in his hideout in the Sangre de Cristo mountains that his sister Teresa had become a saloon singer in Taos and been taken as the mistress of a no-good gambling man. Espinosa had vowed to his mother before she died that he would guard his sister's virtue. There was no time to lose. He and his renegades had swept down across the border into New Mexico, past the 4,000 feet Eagle's Nest, until Taos was in sight.

In his tight leather jacket and velveteen trousers, his finely stitched boots with their cartwheel spurs, Espinosa sat in the saddle, brandished the revolver and shouted, '*Muchachos*! Let's get them!'

He raked his mount's sides and charged before them down towards the unsuspecting town.

★ ★ ★

For three centuries Taos had been a centre for trade and the Spanish influence was strong. A paved plaza was surrounded by a colonnade of adobe buildings dominated by a magnificent mission church. As if to challenge it the American settlers had raised a white-painted, wooden gospel hall at the far end of the dusty street.

However, in Aristide's *cantina*, where most of the heavy drinking and gambling went on, the customers were a mixed bunch, a smattering of *vaqueros* in flared trousers and gaudy shirts in from the outlying *ranchos*, mingling amiably with the *Yanquis*, in their more dowdy homespun suits and felt hats.

It was calm at this time of the afternoon, only the sound of conversation and the clicketing of the ivory ball as it trickled around the spinning roulette wheel. 'Place your bets, *señors*,' the croupier called.

In one corner a poker game was in progress and lounging among the players was a slim, somewhat effete young man, Hal Williams. His fair curly hair hung low over his brow and he was immaculately attired in a grey frock coat, pants to match over polished boots, and a cross-over waistcoat of watered silk. 'I'll see ya,' he muttered, greedily eyeing the pot. He had worked the Mississippi paddle boats and knew he could easily take these hicks for a ride.

On a high stool at the bar sat Teresa, the fiery Mexican girl he had seduced. Her black hair tumbled about her haughty features, her lithe limbs partly exposed by a Spanish off-the-shoulder blouse and a flowing crimson skirt. Her dark eyes were languorous as she watched her lover as if longing for him to finish the game and take her to bed.

For his part, as he glanced at Teresa, it occurred to Hal she was becoming too possessive, watching his every move like a hawk. Maybe it was time he moseyed on to California — on his ownsome.

Outside, Espinosa cautiously slowed his horsemen as they loped into the sunbaked main street, and looked around him. It was languidly peaceful. A few customers in the stores, but most of the citizens were taking a siesta. The Spanish customs died slowly.

'What's this?' The Mexican spied a daguerreo-type likeness of himself on a poster pinned to a tree.

*Wanted, the notorious bandit, Espinosa, charged with murder, kidnapping, rape and robbery, $500 reward, dead or alive.*

'Five hundred?' he scoffed, crumpling the bill in his fist. 'Is that all? They must do better than this.'

He vaulted from his mustang outside Aristide's casino and loose-hitched it to a rail. 'Follow me, men.'

Espinosa pushed apart the batwing

doors and stood on the threshold, accustoming his eyes to the shade, until he spotted Teresa. 'There you are.' He strode across to the bar, snatched hold of her hair, pulled her from the stool and angrily slapped her across her face. 'What have you become? Some *puta* in this bordello?'

Teresa screamed and fought tigerishly with her older brother, but he twisted her arm behind her back and held her across him. 'Where is the stinking dog who has done this to her?'

Hal Williams had spun around in alarm and his bar-room pallor became even more pronounced as he saw the stern-faced bandit and the gruesome array of armed thugs who had taken up positions behind him. It was enough to make even the most stout-hearted man quail.

'Who the hell's this, Teresa?' Hal asked in his soft southern drawl. 'What's going on?'

'Stand up and fight.' Espinosa's fingers touched the butt of his revolver in his belt sash. 'No filthy *gringo* messes with my kin.'

Hal cautiously got to his feet, spreading his hands in a gesture of surrender. 'I ain't armed.' It wasn't exactly true for he had a derringer up the sleeve of his coat. 'I got no fight with you,' he stuttered. 'I ain't hurt her. She came willing. It ain't nuthin' serious 'tween me an' her. Look, you can have my winnings, have my watch, have everything I got. I'll leave town.'

'Shut up. You insult my sister with your words. Give him a gun. Defend yourself, *gringo*.'

'Leave him alone,' Teresa screamed, twisting herself away from her brother's grasp and backing towards Hal, her arms spread to protect him. 'He is no gunfighter. I love him.'

'What?' A look of digust on his face, Espinosa shouted at her, 'How can you? That lousy, cringing dungbeetle. Are you crazy?'

'*Sí.*' Teresa's eyes blazed. 'And he loves me, too.' She turned to the gambler. 'Don't you, Hal?'

'Yes,' he replied, hesitantly. 'I guess I *do*, but — '

'Go.' Teresa spat out. 'Leave us alone. Take those grinning apes with you. You and your so-called *renegados*. Do you think you are still fighting the war?'

'Some of us will never give up,' Espinosa said, swinging his revolver to cover the bar-keep, the roly-poly French proprietor, Aristide, and his varied customers, but none of them appeared eager to challenge him. 'This is our land you have stolen from us. So, I steal what I wan' back from you.'

'If you kill Hal,' Teresa warned, 'you will have to kill me.'

Espinosa scratched his jaw with his free hand. This family encounter was proving more difficult than he imagined. 'Look at you,' he said. 'You think I am going to allow you wait around here like a whore? You disgrace us.'

'Go find a priest, then,' Teresa suggested. 'Hal wants to marry me, don't you, Hal?'

Williams was somewhat reluctant. Marriage had never been among his bag of tricks. But it looked like there was no other way. A shotgun marriage it had to be. 'Sure,' he agreed. 'Of course, I *want* to.'

Espinosa glowered at him. 'Very well. You come with us.'

'What?' Hal was more startled than ever. 'Go with you? Why? Where?'

'Because I say so, gambler. You think I am going to let my sister work in this whorehouse, do you?' Espinosa strode across the floor and went behind the bar intent on pouring himself a glass of tequila. But as he did so the skinny, squeaky-voiced Clarence Dodds, the bar-keep, faced him with a sawn-off shotgun. Whether he panicked, or whether he was braver than he looked, who knows, but Dodd's finger was on the trigger. Hardly deigning to look at him, Espinosa fired his revolver without removing it from the sash on his waist. He leaned back as the shotgun scattered pellets to the ceiling and

Dodds grunted out his last breath as he hit the floor.

'That was a foolish thing to do. I had no argument with him. You saw he tried to kill me.'

Espinosa turned to face the company, raising his tequila before knocking it back. 'Nor any argument with any of you, as long as you do what I say.'

He started taking bottles from the shelves and tossing them to each of his men. 'Save these for the wedding feast tonight.' He opened the till and took what it contained of gold coins and American greenback dollars. 'This will do for us. We wish to make some purchases in your stores then we will be on our way. You gentlemen can carry on with your play.'

He grabbed hold of Teresa's wrist and dragged her with him towards the swing doors. 'Bring the *gringo*,' he called back. 'We will find a priest on the way.'

Espinosa had the arrogance of some slim-hipped matador as he took his time, lit a cigarette, almost inviting any of the Americans to try to kill him. Meanwhile the reluctant bridegroom was frogmarched out of the saloon and put on a mount, alongside Teresa, as the *bandidos* swaggered into the stores, buying sacks of flour, oil for their lanterns, baskets of fruit, strings of peppers, and luxuries like candy and pots of honey. As they paid with Aristide's stolen coin the traders did not protest. They watched the *bandidos* refilling their pouches with bullets and readily provided them with gunpowder and cartridge caps, patches and Miné balls for their rifles.

When they had purloined a couple of mules and loaded up, Espinosa led them at a canter out of town. There was no lawman in Taos and the troopers at Fort Union were a hundred miles away. Few felt inclined to take on the desperados in a gun battle, apart from the livid Aristide, who smashed a window of his saloon and took a potshot at the robbers as they rode off.

He quickly ducked back down as Espinosa swirled his mustang around and returned fire with his revolver, then cantered on his way. A few of the *gringos* came out on to their porches with shotguns and rifles in a half-hearted show of defiance. They dived back into their homes as the bandits turned, riding back and forth, angrily shooting up the town, firing at any who showed their heads.

'You are lucky we do not burn you all down,' Espinosa hollered, shrugging off a bullet that sped past his hat. 'You *gringo* bastards. Beware, or we will be back.'

With which, he spurred his mount, grinned at Teresa, and led them at a fast lope out of town and back north towards the icy fangs of the Rocky mountains.

# 2

Never before had so many emigrants set forth in their trains of covered wagons from the civilized East out across the great plains into the barely mapped regions of the West. That year, 1853, it was estimated that 50,000 had joined the migration.

Seth Tobin, in his buckskin jacket and fringed *chaparejos*, was working as guide, guard and hunter of game for a bunch of wagons owned by the rich trader, Señor Alfredo Almedo, of Santa Fe and Taos. They had made the 600-mile trip to Independence, Missouri, carrying furs and buffalo hides, Navajo jewellery and other artefacts for sale in the East.

They were now returning stacked with canned items and luxury goods which would make a handsome profit for Almedo. One of the prairie schooners was piled high with barrels of whiskey, another with blankets, nails, window frames, tin stoves and so forth. A big Canastoga wagon carried guns and ammunition. In all, it would make a fine prize for marauding Indians, or renegade Mexican bands like Espinosa's, but so far they had had no trouble.

The train of a two-dozen sturdy wagons was pulled by lumbering oxen so progress was slow, if steady.

The mainly Spanish-speaking *sabaneros* were tough and experienced, ready with rifles to rebuff any attack. They were in a merry mood now that the 12,000 foot peaks of the Rockies had appeared out of the haze, flushed pink by the rising sun. Not far to Fort Union and pay-day.

Seth, on his fleet Arab stallion, had decided to scout on ahead to seek a spot with water to camp that night and to shoot an antelope for supper. It would not be a difficult task for there were vast herds of buffalo, intermingled with deer, roaming the plains, as well as a good many wild mustangs.

He must have been about fifteen miles ahead of the wagons when he suddenly saw a spiral of smoke rising up ahead. A shiver up his spine warned him of danger and he halted the stallion to loosen his Paterson .36 five-shot revolver in its holster. His experience indicated the smoke to be a wagon burning. If there was a marauding tribe of Indians about, would it be wise to continue on his own?

He was well armed, a Sharps rifle, with its newly invented breech mechanism for faster loading, slung across his back and plenty of cartridges in the bag on his belt ready for action. Yes, he decided to investigate further.

After a mile or so he came to a narrow creek running away into some scrubby elders from whence the smoke was emanating. Seth slipped from the saddle, ground-hitched the stallion, and stole forward on foot. There were deep ruts in the damp ground, wheel marks, and hoofprints, some shod, but most not. Peering through the branches, sure enough, there was the remains of a charred wagon, still burning. But there was another sight which he had not expected.

Her long blonde hair caught his attention first, flowing down her back almost to her waist, glinting in the sunlight like woven gold. She was turned from him, her limbs, in a worn cotton dress, tensed forward as she wielded the long-handled shovel in her hands. She appeared to have already dug three graves in the sandy earth and was in the act of filling them in.

'Howdy,' he said, in a voice meant to reassure her, stepping out from the bushes.

The girl spun around to face him, swinging the shovel back over her shoulder ready for attack, the look of a young cornered lioness in her poise. Eyes of vivid blue stared at him, defiantly.

'Hey, I ain't gonna hurt ya,' he soothed, holstering the revolver. 'I'm with a wagon train: I saw the smoke.'

She gave a sob and her shoulders slumped in dejection as she let the shovel blade rest on the ground. Seth stepped up close and put his arms around her. 'It's OK. I'm gonna git you outa here.' She suddenly began to shudder, breaking down, letting her head rest against his shoulder, and he felt her tears wetting his shirt. 'OK,' he repeated, patting her back. 'You're safe now. We can't wait around. We gotta make tracks.'

'I'm not leaving until I've buried them.' The girl made an effort to control herself, pulled herself from him, wiping a straggle of hair from her tormented face. She glanced at the bodies of a man, a woman, and a youth, that she had dragged into the shallow graves, and gave a grimace of horror. 'Why do they have to do that?'

'Here, I'll finish filling in.' Seth took the shovel from her. 'If you wanna make crosses, find some string and tie them broken struts from the wagon.'

He took a look at the corpses, steeling himself, although the sight was not unexpected. He had spent a year living with the Shoshone in the north and could have explained that savage custom was to cut out the heart to give them their enemy's strength, and to remove the eyes so they would not be able to recognize them in the Other World. But he guessed that could wait. 'They got their own reasons,' he grunted as he began to work.

She watched him awhile, then went to do as he suggested. They were her mother, her father, and her brother, she explained, as he tamped down the graves, then found rocks to build cairns upon them to keep the wild animals away. She had makeshift crosses ready and he hammered them into the soft ground with the shovel.

Seth paused, the shovel raised, looked around him, sniffing the air, listening. There was the plodding sound of a horse approaching along the creek. His revolver was back in his grip, thumbing the hammer, as he beckoned to her to take cover. He stood his ground, but the horse that appeared was riderless, going at a fast pace, its eyes bulging with fear. Seth jumped and grabbed at its bridle as it tried to charge past. 'Hey, there,' he called, hauling the beast to a halt and calming it. 'Is this'n yourn?'

'My father's saddle horse . . . ' she replied, 'it was.'

'How many wagon hosses?'

'Two. I think they took them.'

'Huccome they didn't take you?'

'I was on that rise,' she said, pointing. 'Picking bilberries from the bushes. First I heard was gunshots, screams, such horrible screams. I stayed hidden until it went quiet.'

'They sure missed a prize.' Seth paused to assess her, the cool, pale Nordic looks, a gal a buck could have had a lot of fun with before selling her for a hundred-dollar rifle to the *comancheros*. 'They'd be kickin' 'emselves iffen they knew.'

The girl, too, looked at the tall, slim-waisted frontiersman as if for the first time. He had cast his wide brimmed hat aside while he worked and he stood, broad-shouldered, wiping sweat from his brow with the back of his hand and tossed his mane of flaxen hair back from his eyes. His grey eyes met hers. 'At least we've got a hoss for ya to ride. That's a blessing.' He pulled a razor-sharp knife and cut a willow switch. 'If I give the word you whack him with every ounce of strength you got and ride like the devil. You can say a few words over your kin, but hurry. I ain't easy in this spot.'

Ruth Simms, she said her name was. She was barefoot, her shapely calves scratched and sunburned. She knelt beside the graves and he saw tears roll down her cheeks again. 'C'mon,' he said, jolting her out of her reverie. He was studying an arrow he had pulled from her mother's breast. 'Looks like Crow. They ain't the nicest to know.'

As she struggled to get a foot in the

stirrup and get on her father's horse, he asked, 'Where's the rest of your party?'

'We were on our own,' she murmured. 'My father got tired of waiting for a wagon train to set out from Independence. He said the Indians were friendly and we could make it to Santa Fe on our own.'

'The Cheyenne and Arapaho might be friendly enough to them who travel together well-guarded. They let us pass. We drop 'em off some sacks of flour and a few knick-knacks now and again to sweeten 'em. But any damn fool who travels on his own is fair game. Your father's only hisself to blame. And, to tell the truth, the Crow hate everybody, white, red or black. C'mon, let's move.'

He planned to ride back the fifteen miles to meet his wagons to warn them. They would probably have seen the smoke by now and have guessed there was a war party on the prowl. What worried him was that the Crow seemed, from what spoor he saw, to have headed back that way, too.

'Aw, shee-it!' he groaned, as they rode out of the elders and started across the grassy prairie for, on a rise up ahead he saw four feathered, painted warriors appear. Crow, sure enough. They paused a few seconds before making their charge, screaming blood-lust as they raised spears and tomahawks and galloped towards them.

'Go!' he roared at her, pointing a finger across the rolling grassland towards the foothills rising in the west. 'Get out. I'll catch up with ya.'

He dropped down into the grass, kneeling with the Sharps hard into his shoulder, taking aim through one squinting eye at the leading Crow in full headdress coming shrieking like a devil out of hell at him. He let him come until he was seventy yards distant. Then squeezed the trigger and dropped him with a chest shot.

The first might be down but the next two didn't hesitate charging like a ball from a cannon straight at him. He lay the single-shot Sharps aside and drew his revolver, supporting it for steady aim across his forearm. He fired and rolled to one side as a lance hissed through the air to thud into the ground where he had just been kneeling. He was back up on his feet, cocking the pistol, and had the brief satisfaction of seeing the lance-warrior doing a back somersault off his war-pony, blood trailing from a shoulder wound. He put another bullet nearer his heart.

'Got him!' he snarled, standing to face an oncoming painted savage in buffalo-horns headmask, who was emitting his gurgling death chant and flailing a razor-sharp tomahawk.

Seth had barely seconds to shoot and jump clear of his horse. But no time to avoid the Indian who hurled himself from the pony and bowled him over, knocking the Paterson from his hand.

He landed in a soggy stream, the near-naked Crow clawing desperately with his left hand to make purchase at his windpipe, stabbing his scalping knife at him. The knife sliced the side of his temple. He jerked his head aside to avoid a repeat blow, gasping for air as the warrior's strong fingers dug into his throat. Somehow he managed to catch hold of his wrist and held the knife at bay. For seconds it was a trial of strength. He could smell the bear-grease in the Crow's black hair, met his murky brown eyes smouldering with hatred and wondered, desperately, what had happened to the fourth warrior.

The knife steadily got nearer and nearer until it was an inch from his throat. The warrior was too heavy for him. He could not hold him. The Crow knew it and his painted face cracked into a leer of triumph. Suddenly, however, it turned into a look of bemused agony as his comrade's lance was hurled thrusting into his back. Its tip protruded with a gush of blood from his chest. He slumped forward and Seth rolled him off into the stream. He looked up to see Ruth standing like some ancient warrior queen, her hair a wild halo of burnished gold, her arm still raised from the release of the iron-tipped lance.

'Jeez!' he cried, struggling up. 'Where'd you come from?'

'I couldn't just leave you.'

'Where's t'other?'

'He's over there.'

A young Indian, not much more than a boy, practically naked but for feathers and loin cloth, a long lance and shield at the ready, was sitting on his pony a hundred yards off, watching.

Seth ran to snatch up his rifle, hurried to get a cartridge into the breech, raised it ready to fire. But the boy was not waiting to be shot from his pony. Instead, he sent it streaking away back across the prairie.

The frontiersman snapped off his shot to no avail and by the time he had another ready the Crow youth was well out of range. 'Dammit! There must be the main war party someplace back there. He's gone to warn 'em. They'll be seeking blood vengeance.'

'You're hurt,' she said, seeing the

blood streaking from his temple.

'Aw, it ain't nuthin'.'

He strode about, examining the bodies of the three Indians to make sure they were dead, searching for his fallen revolver, whistling to the Arab, Star, to come trotting back. 'They'll cut us off from my company. There's no way back. C'mon. We'll have to head fer Fort Union. The faster the better.'

He figured there was another fifteen miles to go to the fort. He slung his Sharps over his back, swung into his own saddle and urged her away.

'Go!' He caught hold of the halter rope of one of the Crow's ponies and took it along with him. It might be a Godsend if her saddle horse gave out. Whatever it was going to be a desperate race for their lives.

# 3

Six uneasy years had passed since United States troops fought their way into the heart of Mexico City. The president, Generalissimo Santa Anna, had fled abroad and vast tracts of territory, Arizona, Texas, New Mexico, California, had been ceded to the *Colussus del Norte*. But Espinosa, for one, had never admitted defeat, never recognized the treachery. He would fight on against the hated *gringos*.

With a forefinger he pushed his sombrero to hang on his broad back and looked out from his eyrie high in the Sangre de Cristo mountains. It had been a successful foray. His heavily laden mules and horses had left Taos and wended their way north along the valley of the infant Rio Grande which, 400 miles due south, would become the newly designated border. Ten miles from Taos at Arroya Seco they had paused to commandeer the village priest and, with a gun in the back of the bridegroom, his sister Teresa had been wed with due ceremony. Espinosa had even bought a virginal white bridal dress for her, although he knew she was not deserving of it. However, their mother would be proud!

On the outskirts of the village they had come across women washing clothes in the stream and the bandit's attention had been caught by the sight of two maidens, their skirts tucked up around their gleaming thighs, who were sporting, with gleeful screams, in the stream.

'Hey,' Espinosa shouted. 'We will have these. Bring them along, *muchachos*.'

The girls' screams had changed from joy to fear as they were scooped up on to the backs of broncos. Another eighty miles on and the *bandidos* abandoned the river and set off across a stretch of vast sand dunes. Espinosa had taken care not to stir the anger of the settlers in Taos. Most of them would find it amusing, he was sure, that they had been paid with the Frenchman Aristide's cash and would not be inclined to raise a posse to follow his cumbersome column. But the desert was a natural barrier which few men cared to cross. Soon he was back on safe ground.

His hideout was an ancient, crumbling tower of stones built by the Capote Utes as a bastion against invasion until they fell back to join their brethren tribes in the mountains on the far side of the Rio Grande, the San Juan range. The tower and its surrounding caves made a fine headquarters for the bandit chief. It was virtually unassailable.

While his men unloaded the packjacks of their booty Espinosa sat on a rock and idly snaked out a bullwhip to tease the two terrified girls. They were bound together with a rawhide rope. Their dark eyes bulged with fear as they cowered mutely before him.

'Don't look so alarmed, *señoritas*,' the Mexican called, as he toyed with them sadistically. 'Tonight you discover the joy of being chosen by Espinosa. Then I will throw you to my dogs.'

He laughed harshly, cracked the whip to make the nervous creatures jump, and shouted at some old crones he kept as camp followers to serve them. '*Hola*! Isn't that ready yet?' They were roasting a mountain sheep on a spit. 'Pile on more wood. I am starving. We have had a long ride.'

'Have patience,' one of the black-clothed women squawked. 'This is a tough old ram. He needs to be well-grilled.'

Espinosa's 'dogs' had begun to carouse for he had bade them make a start on the bottles of whiskey and tequila and break open a cask of wine.

A giant of a man known as *El Borracho*, the drunkard, was raising a stout barrel high in his muscular arms and attempting to drink the wine that gushed from the spigot.

'Hey, you pig,' Espinosa cried. 'Don't hog it all. Fill my mug. Careful! You are spilling it. Give some to the *Americano*. This is his wedding breakfast we celebrate. Hey, brother-in-law, how you like being wed?'

His fine clothes grimed with dust, Hal Williams was not at all happy about his situation. He was exhausted from the long two-day ride under the fierce sun and fearful of what these uncouth, armed-to-the-teeth brutes planned to do with him. He sat despondently on a discarded saddle and tried to give a brave smile as *El Borracho* splashed wine for him. He caught as much as he could in a clay mug and raised it in salute. 'It ain't exactly what I had in mind.'

'What? You ungrateful cur, you have my beautiful sister as your bride, you have all the wine and food you want; you can ride free with my merry band; what more do you need?'

'What do you expect Hal to say, you bully?' Teresa, who was still in her white wedding dress, shrieked. 'What right have you to tell us how to live our lives?'

Espinosa ignored her, mockingly raising his mug of wine to the *Americano*. 'So, how you like my hideout? You don' wan' ride with us?'

Williams looked dolefully at his wine and took a gulp. 'It seems OK, but not what you might call civilized.'

'You say we not civilized?' Espinosa demanded of the pale-eyed *Americano*. 'What do you say, that we are animals? We are brutes?'

'No, not at all,' Hal stuttered, lighting a slim cheroot and watching Teresa, who was helping the women, down on her knees by the smoky fire. 'It's not just my way of life, that's all. I'm more an indoors man.'

Espinosa braced himself, pushing fingers back through his thick black curls, and spat into the dust. He did not like the look of this limp-wristed *gringo* one little bit and was puzzled by what his sister saw in him. But women often fell for men of his sort. Surely she knew he had no backbone, no grit.

'We seem OK to you, huh?' he growled in his broken English. 'That all you got to say?'

'No.' Hal Williams sucked nervously at the cheroot and blew out smoke. 'I just don't understand why you've brought me here, that's all.'

'Why?' Espinosa bellowed. 'You don' know why? I tell you why, because Teresa must not disgrace my family. May God help you if you ever think of abandoning or harming her.'

Hal gulped visibly, swallowing his alarm. 'Sure, that's fine by me. But we would be happier in Taos together. That's how I earn my crust, gambling. I'm not cut out for this kind of thing. You surely don't expect me to ride with you?'

'This kind of thing!' Espinosa gave a shrill laugh as he repeated the words. He drew his long-barrelled revolver, pointed it at the American, then swung his arm to fire between the heads of the two startled Latino girls. The bullet hit the rocks and went whining and ricocheting away. 'You hear that, *amigos*? The *gringo*'s not cut out for thieving, killing, raping. He prefers to linger like some pale slug under a stone.' Another bullet whined past Williams's boot, making him jump with alarm.

His men grinned blackened teeth and joined in roars of gruff laughter as Teresa sprang like a tigress to defend her cub. She stood in front of Williams and hissed at her brother, 'You leave him alone. He is my man. You will not harm him.'

'Sister,' Espinosa smiled, 'why should I want to harm your husband? He is one of *us*.'

For moments Teresa looked nonplussed, then tugged at her wedding dress that had slipped from one shoulder and tossed her hair, arrogantly. 'Just remember what I say. And cut the bonds of those girls. Give them a drink. The poor creatures are exhausted.'

'You hear what she says,' Espinosa

yelled, spinning his revolver on one finger and returning it to his holster. 'Give them wine. Cut them free. I want to see them dancing. I want to hear them singing. I want them in the mood for loving. Tonight the foolish virgins will discover what a man Espinosa is. Then tomorrow, my *renegados*, you can have them.'

He cackled with laughter as the two dark-hued girls stood before him, easing their wrists released from the rawhide, staring at him, mute with terror. He picked up his whip and lashed its lead tip to crack at their bare toes.

'Go on! Dance! Dance for Espinosa.'

'That might not be such a good idea,' Hal Williams protested.

'What?' The bandit chief got to his feet, his raw-hide six-foot snake raised. 'Who are you to tell me—?'

'I happen to know those two aren't just common peasant girls. I have seen their father bring them into Taos.'

'What you talk about?'

'I tell you, their father might not have much cash himself. Just a small rancher. Maybe you think he can do nothing about you taking his daughters, but, like I say, I happen to know his brother is a very rich merchant in Taos. Señor Almedo would be honour bound to pay a ransom for his nieces.'

For the first time Espinosa appeared surprised by the words of the Yankee. 'Maybe you know more than I gave you credit for. Maybe you are not just a spineless slug of a gambler who has seduced my sister.'

'Maybe I'm not. To tell you the truth I don't give a damn what you do with the poor kids, but personally I think you would be making a mistake if you ill-treat them. Señor Almedo is an astute businessman and he would expect to get his brother's girls back in good condition. He ain't gonna pay for damaged goods.'

'Sí?' Espinosa's face took on a wolfish look, then he flashed a grin. 'How much you think he pay?'

Hal tossed his hair back from his eyes and shrugged. 'Who knows, maybe five thousand dollars in gold. The best thing would be for me to go back and discuss it with him.'

'*Hai*!' Espinosa gave a yelp of disbelief. 'We let you go and we no see you again for dust, you crafty Yankee dog.'

The gambler's pale-blue eyes met the dark fiery ones of the Mexican and he, too, smiled. 'Look at these hands,' he said. 'They are the tools of my trade, the only trade I know. I need them to remain soft as a baby's bottom. I need to know the touch of every card in the deck when I run my fingers over them. Look, all this rough riding ain't doing them any good. Already I'm getting callouses. What's the point of keeping me a prisoner in these mountains? I would be more use to you in Taos. I visit the big houses. I listen. I know what's going on, when any big pay-offs will be carried.'

'What you mean,' Espinosa sneered. 'Pay-offs?'

'You must know Señor Almedo is an important trader. He ships freight in from the East. He gets a big pay-off, I can assure you. I've heard he often carries ten thousand dollars in his belt when he returns to Taos to stock up for more peltry ready for the next trip.'

'You don' say?' Espinosa stroked his unshaven jaw, then gave his fanatical laugh. 'He sounds a bigger bandit than me.'

'Maybe,' Hal smiled. 'The big difference is he ain't likely to git hanged for *his* cheatin' ways.'

'Pah! All you want is for me to free you so you can run away and save your skin. I know your worthless sort. Your wedding vows mean nothing to you. You will abandon my sister at the first opportunity.'

'That's not true: I love her,' the gambler protested. He had always been an adept liar. He put an arm around Teresa. 'All I want is to get back to Taos.' Mainly, it occurred to him, so he could get a hot bath and a clean suit of clothes.

'What is the matter with you, Brother?' the girl spat out. 'You don't want me to spend my married life in these lousy caves, do you? Now I am married I want it to be the real thing. Like Hal says, we'd be much better for you working on the inside.'

'OK.' Espinosa's face lit up. 'Maybe you speak the truth. You can both leave in the morning, but I will be sending three of my best men along to keep an eye on you. You arrange the ransom for these two' — he flicked the whip disdainfully at the girls — 'you send me word and the exchange will be arranged.'

'It's a done deal.' Hal grinned and stuck out his hand. 'Shake on it, Brother-in-law.'

Espinosa crushed his fingers in an iron grip. 'Be warned. You try to doublecross me . . . these hands would hold no more cards. I would slice them off.'

'I don' wanna cheat you, but I'm in

this for the cash, too. I'm willing to go into partnership with you. What's my cut? Twenty per cent?'

'No. I will give you ten per cent of what you get.'

'Fair enough. Maybe we'll have another shot of that tequila, eh, Teresa? Your charming pig of a brother can toast the happy couple.'

'Theenk yourself lucky,' Espinosa growled, 'I do not toast you over the flames, Senor Williams.'

'Call me Hal. Yeah, let's have a party.' Suddenly bouyant with success, the American yelled, 'Here's to a profitable future, Espinosa, old pal.'

He squeezed alcohol spurting from a goatskin to catch in his mouth. 'Ain't that meat done yet, Teresa? Tell them old hags to hurry it along. I'm damn well starved, too.'

'So now the *gringos* giving orders?' Espinosa snapped his whip at *El Borracho* who was stumbling about trying to make the two Latino girls dance. 'Leave them alone. There's been a change of plan. Those two are not on the menu tonight. We have to keep them pure for their rich uncle.'

What did it matter? There were plenty of dark-skinned peasant girls they could pluck. What he would really like, he mused, would be to get his hands on some beautiful white-skinned *Americano* girl. Alas, they were few and far between. But that would be a prize worth the taking. He would not surrender her so readily.

# 4

'Riders coming!' was the halloo from the look-out at Fort Union. 'Indian attack!'

Sergeant-Major Pat Murphy ceased square-bashing his bevy of new recruits and bellowed, 'Sound the alarm. Here's your chance, boyos, for a taste of action. Get to your posts.'

Soldiers ran to clamber up to the walkway on the twenty-foot high adobe-and-brick walls, long-barrelled Springfields at the ready and watched as a long-legged youngster on a white Arab stallion came at the gallop towards them, followed by what appeared to be a golden-haired girl on an Indian pony hard on his heels. A bunch of screaming Crow were in fast pursuit.

Captain George Ravilious, in his ostrich-plumed campaign hat and scarlet bandanna, peered through his telescope and shouted, 'Open the gates and be ready to close 'em quick again.'

The captain was a bit of a cavalier, with his long locks and cavalry jacket specially tailored in best blue worsted, adorned with gilt braids of rank, and his high boots.

'Well, I'll be damned!' he exclaimed. 'What a looker! She certainly knows how to ride. Where on earth did she spring from?'

He examined the girl through the glass, a slim figure, slashing at the pony's hide, valiantly urging it on as it charged towards the fort. She rode astride, her dress rucked up revealing her shapely thighs as they gripped the pony's sides, the wind sending her long hair rippling behind her.

'Anybody'd larn to ride fast with them devils on their heels,' his sergeant growled. 'Prepare to fire, men. Choose ya targets.'

There was a look of panic and desperation on the girl's face as her sturdy buffalo pony carried her towards them. Her companion wheeled his stallion to await her, raising his arm to fire a revolver shot at the flood of forty savages crying for blood less than a hundred yards off now. He urged the girl on and sped behind her towards the open gates.

'Fire!' Muskets roared in unison, but as most of the raw recruits couldn't hit a barn door at twenty paces, their lead did little harm. A ball from the more experienced Murphy did, however, dislodge one feathered warrior from his pony, and all in all the fusillade sufficed to deter the invaders as Seth and Ruth reached safety and the gates were slammed shut.

With howls of wrath at losing their prey after such a close-run race, the Crow picked up the dead man, and retreated to a safer distance, where they contented themselves with gesticulating in a rude manner and hurling abuse, fortunately not easily understandable.

'Reload,' Murphy ordered and the recruits primed their muzzle-loaders.

'Prepare to fire.' Another volley barked out. 'There! That's set 'em off, sor.'

But Ravilious wasn't listening. His attention was riveted on the girl. In fact, he was stymied by the sight of her. What a gorgeous creature! He hurriedly descended the ladder to welcome her to the fort.

Some of the Crow were firing their ancient *fusées* or trade muskets at the fort, but it was a mere show. After some talk among themselves they decamped and set off back into the prairie, soon to become just a spiral of dust disappearing into the unknown.

'Ye did well, my brave boys,' Sergeant Murphy shouted. 'Ye're getting the hang of them muskets. Back to the parade ground. We may have to go in pursuit of the hostiles.'

Captain Ravilious had commandeered the girl and was ushering her towards his office with promise of refreshment. She glanced back at Seth as he watched her go, but he was buttonholed by his employer, Señor

Almedo, who wanted to know just why he had abandoned his wagon train.

'Ah, sure, I don't think them cowardly Crow will attack the wagons. They're after easier game. And, if they do, your *sabaneros* will be a match for 'em. Don't worry, I'll ride back to meet 'em as soon as Star has got back his breath. We've had a wild ride for fifteen miles and it was touch and go the last five when they got on our tails. I was worried about the safety of the girl.'

Alfredo Almedo was a tall, haughty Latino, attired Mexican-style in a tight-hipped, pearl-embroidered suit. He was rumoured to be the richest man in the territory. He led Seth to the sutler's store, situated alongside the livery and wheel-wright beneath the ramparts.

'I'll pay you now,' he said going into his office, sitting himself at a table in one corner and taking a handful of gold coins from a wooden casket which he passed across. 'I've got another assignment for you.'

Seth took the $100 for two months away on the trail. Normally, he would have been content, but another such job was not on his agenda. 'I ain't fer hire no more,' he drawled, slipping the coins into the ammunition pouch on his belt.

Almedo was busy scratching with a quill pen at figures in his accounts book. 'You've got the barrels of whiskey I ordered? Right, I want half to go on to Santa Fe and half to Albuquerque. I'll trust you to collect payment. Then, the army is looking for us to make another trip to collect supplies and gun parts. You've done well. I'm pleased with you.'

'You didn't seem to hear me, *señor*. I'm sorry, but I got other plans.'

'What? Don't be ridiculous. I'll make you wagon master. You choose the route, you control the men, you'll be in charge of the whole caboodle, my major domo. It'll mean a pay rise of fifty dollars.'

'It's like this, Alfredo.' Seth poured himself a tequila and took a bite of lemon and a touch of salt. He lounged back in a chair opposite him and reminisced. 'I been working for other men since I was a kid of thirteen when I first came out to this country. Don't know whether I've told you afore, but my parents were both dead and I got a job as greaser' — greasing the wheels of the wagons — 'with a party coming out of Missouri. Walked practically the whole damn way. Then Uncle Dick hired me to go on a trapping expedition through the Rockies. We were away two years, went thousands of miles, returned loaded with peltry. He made a big pile of dollars. All I received was a handful of silver. I ain't complainin'; I was just a kid. It was the greatest experience of my life. Wouldn't have missed it. But it's been the same thing ever since. I've been hunter, guide, 'puncher, drover, gold panner, army scout, working hard, putting my life on the line. What have I got to show for it? Not a lot. So, I've decided to go into business on my own account. If you can do it, so can I.'

'Don't kid yourself, Seth,' Almedo muttered, as he scratched with the quill. 'Running a business is not as easy as it might appear.' He tossed away the pen and stretched back, running long fingers through his silver hair. For a man in his late fifties he was hard and lean from years spent in the saddle. 'You need more experience. Have you got a head for figures? Can you organize, delegate, make deals? I keep it all in my head, up here. I have earned the trust of business colleagues, even of your government. Well, I suppose it is my government since the war between our countries, as I am now, like it or not, a citizen of the United States.'

'I intend to try,' Seth replied. 'I ain't looking to make as much as you. What have you got, this big teamster business, twenty-three wagons, hundreds of mules, oxen and hosses. A mansion in Santa Fe, another in Taos. That magnificent ranch outside Taos your son runs for you. Fingers in God knows how many pies. All that gold stashed away. Yes, don't deny it. That's what folks say, anyhow.'

Almedo lit a slim cigar impassively, blew out a ring of smoke, and asked, 'What are you looking for, Seth?'

The young man shrugged his broad shoulders. 'Just enough to buy me a piece of land, raise horses and cattle, put down roots, maybe marry me a purty gal; who knows, have sons, like you. That's all. I ain't overly ambitious.'

'So, how do you plan to start making money?'

Seth grinned. 'By going into competition with you, starting my own teamster business. I plan to be based in Taos, make runs up to the mines in the hills, or down to Santa Fe to collect goods, whatever's on offer. I'm going into partnership. Maybe we'll start a stage line once we git organized.'

'Who's your partner?'

'That's my business. We still got to shake on it. That's why I gotta go up to Taos to clinch the deal.'

'Ah, you're getting secretive. This filly

you arrived with wouldn't have any-thing to do with your decision, would she? You wouldn't be trying to impress her?'

'Nope. My partner's been getting things together, buying wagons and horses while I've been away on this trip. At least,' he muttered, more to himself, 'I hope he has.'

'*Sí*, you hope.' Señor Almedo smiled and leaned across to offer his hand. 'You should bet on certainty, not hope. But if your mind is made up, I wish you well.'

'Fine.' Seth returned the handshake and stood. 'Guess I'll go git Star an' we'll head out to meet the boys.'

A trumpet was sounding. A platoon of troopers was saddling up ready to go out on patrol. Seth joined the officer at the head of the column, and, with the Stars and Stripes fluttering in the breeze, they set off out on to the prairie. Not that they had much chance of catching up with the Crow now but it would be some sort of show and at least ensure protection for his comrades.

*   *   *

Captain Ravilious was more concerned about protecting the crate of brandy he had ordered from Almedo. Ruth was being taken care of by the officers' wives, who would bathe her and find her a decent dress. She would need to rest after her ordeal. But she was a spritely body and should be recovered by the morrow.

When the wagon train arrived with eastern delicacies, he planned to hold a party in the officers' mess, with the fort's musicians on hand. And guess who would be leading the winsome blonde beauty in the dancing? Yes, the handsome George Ravilious. He could hardly wait and busied himself planning the menu and the musical numbers.

Once the wagons had lumbered in the next evening the captain paid particular care preening himself before his mirror, curling his hair and moustache ends, splashing perfume on his shaven cheeks, donning a fine white linen shirt, which he wore neck open to display his bronzed chest. Commanding Officers were allowed to take liberties with their appearance and he pulled on a light blue jacket with epaulettes, wore his tightest nankeen trousers to display his manly rider's thighs, pulled on his highly-polished boots and strapped tight his dragoon sabre, its point tipping the ground.

'How do I look?' he asked Murphy.

'A foine sight, sor,' the sergeant grunted. 'A foine sight, indeed. Ye'll set the ladies' hearts aflutter.'

Ravilious poured him a shot of brandy. 'Good man. Everything's prepared as I ordered, is it?'

'It is indeed, sor.' Murphy clicked his heels and raised the brandy. 'A jolly night it should be.'

'Yes, well, I've got to go careful with this stuff. That rogue Almedo charged me two-fifty a bottle. I bet he got it for a dollar a bottle back in Independence.'

'He has to make his profit, sor.'

'Right, Sergeant-Major, lead on.'

In his own version of dress uniform, pill box hat, white gautlets and his best jacket, Murphy strutted before him to the mess hall where the officers and wives were assembled. Not that there were many of them, just the surgeon and his ancient spouse, the commander of artillery, a melancholy former major who had been reduced to infantry captain as a result of some unfortunate business with a fellow officer's wife, and a couple of brash second lieutenants fresh out from West Point. One of these, Lt Phipps, had his wan, newly wed wife hanging on his arm.

Captain Ravilious's arrival was announced by Murphy in a parade-ground bellow and he took centre stage as punch was dispensed from a silver bowl. 'Ah, Miss Simms,' he cried, cornering the new arrival who looked quite stunning in a borrowed white dress. 'Or may I call you Ruth? Will you do me the honour of sitting on my right? We have a treat in store. You'll be surprised.'

Dinner was announced and it was, indeed a feast. Oyster pie, grilled trout, venison steak and sweet potatoes, all kinds of cream puddings and fruit, wine, coffee, pastries. Ruth watched them all digging in with gusto. They certainly knew how to live high on the hog. It was quite amazing after the fare she'd been used to.

'Drink up,' the captain urged, topping up her wine glass. 'You've had a nasty experience. Need to build up your strength. Think of the future now.'

'What has happened to Seth?' she asked. 'Isn't he invited to join us?'

'Quite out of the question, dear girl.' Ravilious patted her hand. 'What, a wagon-train scout in the officers' mess? It's just not done. Why so interested in him?'

Ruth shrugged. 'I just wanted to thank him for saving my life.'

'From what I heard you saved his. Killed that Indian. You were very brave,

Ruth.' This time his hand had slid under the table and patted her thigh. 'A very brave girl, indeed.'

Ruth flinched at the touch and nearly spilt her wine. 'I'd rather you didn't do that, Captain,' she gritted out.

Ravilious grinned, but obeyed. By the time she'd been plied with more punch she might not be so hoighty-toighty.

'You say your father was a carpenter? A useful trade. But trade nonetheless. So, I'm making an exception here for you. You should be honoured, my dear.'

Ruth didn't much like the sound of this, but Captain Ravilious had turned from her and was discussing army business in stentorian tones.

'There's been trouble at Taos,' he announced. 'A messenger has come in. One man shot by the bandit Espinosa, the saloon-keeper robbed. The citizens are demanding a punitive expedition. This on top of the massacre at Pueblo.'

He turned back to Ruth, twirling his moustachios, and explained, 'Twenty Latinos slaughtered when the Utes tricked their way into the fort saying they wanted to trade. Mexicans, Indians, you can't trust any of 'em. No need for alarm, but how the government expects us to police this vast wilderness with a few ill-armed men from a scattering of far and wide forts, God only knows.'

In a lower tone he explained to Ruth, dipping his head close to hers, that he understood her only relative was an uncle living in Taos, so he would combine business with pleasure and personally escort her to safety there.

'Meanwhile,' he cried, jumping up, 'the night is young. Shall we dance?'

Ruth could hardly say no as the dashing captain took her hands and the military band struck up 'My darling, Clementine'. He led her out on to the floor and into a waltz. Indeed, the first of many reels, jigs, squares until Ruth's head was spinning and she was quite exhausted. By the way he whooped and whirled her around you would imagine Ravilious thought they were the only couple on the floor.

'Sit down, my dear, and catch your breath,' Mrs Phipps cooed as the captain went off for more glasses of punch. 'Captain Ravilious is running you off your feet.'

'Yes, I am in a bit of a whirl.' Ruth groaned at the sight of Ravilious returning with brimming glasses. 'Oh, no, not again.'

When she made an excuse of a headache, the captain frowned, but offered to escort her back to her room. In the darkness outside he suddenly caught hold of her with demonic force and began showering her with kisses. She had more or less to fight him off.

Luckily he had to desist when Mrs Phipps arrived saying that she, too, was feeling faint and in need of smelling salts. Ravilious was forced to bid a curt goodnight and return to the shindig. 'That woman,' he muttered, 'always poking her nose in. Still, early days yet.'

'Be careful, my dear,' young Mrs Phipps hissed, before slipping from

Ruth's room. 'A girl's only beacon of light in this lawless and Godless country is chastity. Don't let Captain Ravilious . . . well, you know what I mean.'

Ruth sat on her bunk, brushing her long hair, listening to the distant sound of martial music. Yes, she knew what Mrs Phipps implied. The captain was a very persuasive man. But how was she to quell his ardour without offending him? 'Oh, well,' she sighed, 'I guess I'm just lucky to be alive.'

# 5

El Borracho and his two *compañeros* rode quietly into the dusty, sunbaked streets of Taos with Hal Williams and the tempestuous Teresa on mustangs beside them.

'You lie low here,' Hal called, nodding towards a low-slung, adobe *cantina* frequented by Latinos. 'We'll go see if we can find Almedo.'

'Don't go getting drunk and causing trouble, you oaf,' Teresa warned *El Borracho*.

The giant Mexican grinned through his heavy moustache, swinging down from his mount and pointing a finger at her. 'All you got to do is get a good price for those girls. Don't keep us waiting too long. Your brother may get impatient.'

'We'll be as quick as we can,' Hal said, riding on towards Aristide's casino.

There was no great danger here for the three *bandidos* unless they started causing mayhem and the white settlers took the law into their own hands. So best keep them away from the scene of their crime where the *gringos* congregated. Hal was keen to get the ransom arranged, pocket some gold and return to his natural habitat, a poker game.

'You're back!' Aristide seemed surprised to see him. They let you go?'

'Yeah,' Hal drawled, calling for a bottle of champagne. 'Just as soon as they made sure we was wed.'

'Ha!' A smile spread over the corpulent Frenchman's face as he thumbed out the stopper and poured two glasses of the bubbly cooled by ice brought down from the mountains. 'Never thought I'd see you nailed. But here's to you both. It's on the house.'

'You seem remarkably cheerful for a man who was robbed and his best bar-keep shot,' the Mexican girl remarked.

'Ach, I am a professional man. I will recoup my losses.' Aristide raised a glass to Teresa. 'But if that bastard brother of yours ever steps in here again it will be the last thing he does.'

'Is Almedo around?' Hal asked.

'No, he's down at Fort Union.'

'A pity, I got urgent business with him.'

'He should be back soon,' Aristide replied. 'If not we'll be running out of whiskey.'

'In that case I'll go get myself a shave and bath at the barber shop and some clean duds,' Hal said. 'I'll see you back at the hotel, honey. Bring another bottle. I'm in a loving mood.'

'Are you coming back as my cabaret girl?' Aristide asked Teresa, plonking another bottle on the counter for her.

'No, I'm afraid not. My brother does not approve. He thinks the little wife should stay home and behave herself.'

'In that case you have to pay for this one. A dollar fifty to you. Any news on those two girls Espinosa snatched? Everybody fears the worst.'

'They're OK. He has promised not to

harm them. That's what we want to see Señor Almedo about. We think we can arrange their safe return.'

'At a price?'

'Well,' she shrugged. 'Nobody does anything for nothing in this world. You should know that.'

★ ★ ★

Captain Ravilious had decreed that the platoon of cavalry should remain at the fort to patrol the plain, while he led their company of infantry up to Taos. They dismantled a twelve-pound howitzer to carry on three pack mules. It would be a hard trail up to the plateau, taking a zig-zag route winding up the rocky mountainside. Of course, he rode his own charger himself but, like their guide Seth Tobin, was often forced to step down and proceed on foot.

Señor Almedo, after dispatching his wagons to Santa Fe the long way round through the Glorietta Pass, decided to take advantage of army protection and go with them with his *burros* loaded with barrels and bales to Taos. Maybe the sight of the golden-haired girl on her Indian pony affected his decision.

It was good to get away from the stultifying heat of the plain and gradually reach cooler altitudes amid piñon trees, bubbling streams, flower-filled meadows where bears were a common sight as they feasted on berries, and the eagle soared.

'It's quite beautiful,' she cried as she saw the snowy peaks of the Rockies in the distance against a clear blue sky.

'It's fine in the summer,' Ravilious replied, 'but not many folk wait around in the hills once the winter snows arrive. Apart from foolhardy backwoods mountain men like your friend Tobin.'

Ruth looked across at Seth and smiled, but she didn't get much chance of talking to him as the captain and Alfredo Almedo rode either side of her and commandeered the conversation. Behind them trudged the infantry to the sound of flute and drummer boy, while the creaking of harness and the bells on the necks of the pack-jacks carried to them on the mountain breeze.

Ruth was surprised by the courtly attention paid to her by the lean and wiry Señor Almedo, with his wavy grey hair beneath his sombrero and his old Spanish manners. 'You must allow me to visit you at Taos,' he insisted. 'I will take you out driving in my coach. You will love it.'

The girl was not so sure that she would. He was old enough to be her father and, apparently, a widower. The fierceness of his regard her way and his ornate flattery seemed more than fatherly. All in all she was glad when they sighted Taos, although apprehensive of what sort of reception she would get at her uncle's house. Would he welcome her or not?

★　★　★

'Hey, *amigos* what have we here?' *El Borracho* gave a groan of appreciation as he saw the lissom girl, with golden hair streaming down to her mid-back, riding the painted pony as the column of infantry and *burros* trailed into Taos. 'Look at that angel. Where has she come from?'

One of his companions, the razor-faced Miguel, brandished his fist in the air and grunted, 'I don't know where she come from but I know where I want to take her.'

'*Whupa!*' howled the third *bandido*, his expressive yell accompanied by a string of remarks not easily translatable in polite society.

They were sprawled in the shade of a colonnade and in their greasy *vaquero* garb hardly given a glance by Captain Ravilious and the others as they cantered into the plaza.

'The good Lord smiles down on us today.' *El Borracho* slapped the heavy Volcanic pistol stuck in his belt. 'He has sent us this beauty. We must have her.'

'What about Espinosa?' Gustavo cautioned.

'*Sí.*' *El Borracho* grinned brown, broken teeth. 'He can have her — after we have finished with her.'

\* \* \*

Alfredo Almedo made a fastidious farewell to Ruth before hurrying away to attend to business. Captain Ravilious was much occupied in finding billets for his officers and a spot for his men to pitch their pup tents. So Seth took the opportunity of showing the girl the whereabouts of her uncle's emporium.

'He's a bit of a miserable old buzzard, I guess I oughta warn ya,' he said. 'But he's done well since he arrived here. Mainly by cheatin' folks outa their last cent.'

'Please,' she begged, her blue eyes blazing into his. 'Stay and give me moral support; explain to him what happened.'

'Waal, I oughta be on my way,' Seth eyed Aristide's saloon wistfully. 'I'd like to cut the dust from my throat first.

But, sure, why not?'

He hitched his stallion outside the store and jumped on to the sidewalk. 'Come on.'

In the shade of the canopy Ruth hesitated and grasped his strong sun-burned wrist. 'Before we go in,' she said, 'I ain't had much chance of talking to you, but I want to thank you for everything. Will I see you again?'

'You betcha, gal.' He squeezed her hand and met her eyes. 'But I gotta go up into the hills to Cañon City to see what that no-good pardner of mine is up to. I wanna try and make somethang of myself, Ruth. I'll be back soon. Ya don't think I'm gonna leave you to these wolves.'

'You mean the captain?'

'Yep, an' that lecherous ol' Spaniard.'

She smiled at him. 'They're nothin' to me.'

'They got cash an' that's what most gals look fer in a man.'

'Not always.'

'Yeah, well, we'll see,' he replied,

somewhat bitterly. 'C'mon, let's meet the gang.'

He pushed open the glass-fronted door and called out, 'Hey, look who's here. You got a visitor.'

A skeletal, bald-domed man poked his head out through some baskets of musty fruit and squinted at them through a pince-nez. 'What in tarnation you want?' he squawked.

'It's your brother's gal. Nearly lost her lovely hair to the Crow. She's had a terrible time getting here.'

Three soft and silly girls arrived from the back room. 'Here's ya cousin Ruth,' he said, pushing her towards them. 'Ain't ya gonna give her a hug and a kiss?'

★　★　★

Ezekiel Simms's store was piled high with food-stuffs and general habadashery. When his wife Mildred wasn't serving in the store she and her daughters spent their days in a back room sewing dresses copied from the fashions in out-of-date magazines. While she fussed about the new arrival Ezekeil's eyes in his skull-like face were icily cold, perhaps assessing how much another mouth eating his vittles would cost him. But by the Western customs of blood and hospitality he was bound to take the girl in.

'Right,' he snapped, 'perhaps we can get back to our supper now.'

Seth was inveighed upon to stay and more out of curiosity he agreed. It was obvious that Ezekiel demanded total obedience from his wife and daughters and after saying grace he set to slurping at his bowl of onion soup to indicate the meal had begun. Supper was generally passed in a silence like the grave.

Unaware of this, Ruth asked the oldest girl, Rebecca, 'What do you do here in the evenings? Take a promenade around the town square?'

Ezekiel frowned at her, spoon poised. 'They certainly do not. They git on with their chores or study the Bible.'

Seth grinned at the spotty-faced sisters. 'Ain't you interested in gittin' such charming young leddies wed?'

Rebecca stifled a giggle and her plump, pasty cheeks blushed scarlet. Her father quickly intervened. 'No I ain't. Certainly not to the likes of you. When the time comes we'll find 'em suitable suitors. Meantime they earn their keep and Cousin Ruth will have to as well.'

Seth stroked back his fawn hair from his eyes and gave the girls a wink. With his buckskin jacket and fringed chaps he guessed he did look a bit of a backwoodsman. His drawl, picked up among the mountain men, didn't help much, either. 'Lucky gals,' he muttered.

Ezekiel returned to sucking at his soup and announced, 'That brother of mine allus was a fool. Fancy him goin' an' gittin' hisself killed and his wife and son, too.'

'That wasn't his intention,' Ruth replied fiercely, wondering how two brothers could be so poles apart.

71

The girls swivelled their eyes at her. It wasn't advisable to answer back to their father. But his wife, Mildred, her face as pinched and pained as her husband's, kept her eyes down. If ever women were cock-pecked, Seth thought, it was this crowd.

'Why didn't he stick with a reg'lar wagon train? Trust him to think he could go it alone.' That appeared to be Simms's verdict on the tragedy. 'So now we gotta pick up the pieces and look after this hussy. Well, I trust she ain't bringing any of her feisty Eastern ways into this house.'

He beckoned to Rebecca to start clearing the plates and bring in the meat course. 'As if I ain't got enough females gettin' under my feet without havin' to take on another one.'

Simms, himself, had headed West three years before with his young family intending to try to make his fortune in the California gold rush of '49. But he had joined the wrong wagon train and instead of taking the Oregon trail to

Fort Hall and the cut-off through the Rockies blazed by Jedediah Smith to Sacramento, he had found himself on the Santa Fe trail. He hadn't realized this until they had crossed the great plains and reached Fort Union.

'The Lord guided my steps to Santa Fe and on north to this town and commanded me to put down roots,' he said. 'If your father had paid more attention to his prayers he might have prospered as I have.'

'Yes, perhaps,' Ruth commented, icily, as she surveyed the razor-thin slices of beef and watery slop of potatoes that were being served. 'Perhaps not.'

'Might I remind you, young lady, that we pay strict observance to our Baptist religion in this household. I'd like you to be aware of that. Also you will have your hair cut and be dressed in more modest style from here on. I don't know what you have been up to with this young fella out in the wilderness on your own, but I doubt it's been beneficial for your soul.'

'I think,' Ruth said, 'my soul can take care of itself. And, to tell the truth, I like my hair as it is.'

Seth grinned and urged, 'That's right, you tell him, gal. Seems to me like this scrawny buzzard needs someone to twist his nose.'

'You keep out of this, mister.' Ezekiel waggled a finger at him and then at Ruth. 'Let me make it quite clear. If any of my daughters, or you, niece, should bring dishonour on us — you're old enough to know what I'm talking about — be quite sure you know the punishment: to be expelled from this house. The only other living you'll find will be in a whorehouse.'

'Father!' For once even his wife was moved to express her shock. 'Such language!'

'I'm sorry, Mildred, but I must call a spade a spade. I won't say more, but they must be fully aware of the consequences of ungodly behaviour.'

Seth raised his eyebrows at Ruth and

grinned, 'So, now you know, gal.' He slapped his napkin down on the table and glanced around the sparsely furnished cabin behind the store. 'Just watch your step and do what you're told and you'll be OK. Sure saves me havin' to lock a chastity belt on you while I'm away.' He scraped his chair back and got to his feet. 'Waal, I must be on my way. I sure hate to leave such a cheery bunch, but you know how it is. So long, folks. I'll call in again, Simms, if I'm back this way an' see how your pupil's progressin'.'

'Ruth!' Ezekiel ordered. 'He can find his own way out.'

But the girl disobeyed him, lightly springing to her feet and following Seth out to the front door. 'I'm going to miss you,' she whispered.

'I never knew a body could slice beef so thin. Still, at least you won't be putting any meat on.' Seth smiled at her, coiled an arm around her waist and gently kissed her lips. 'Bear up, gal. It may be cold comfort here, but, like he says, it's better than being out on the street.'

'I'm not so sure of that.'

She hung onto his fingertips until he pulled away and jumped from the sidewalk on to the saddle of the Arab. He jerked the reins free and set the cream-coloured stallion prancing and almost dancing in a circle. 'So long, honey,' he called. 'Don't forget to say your prayers. I'll be heading north in the morning.'

'Where you going now?'

'Guess.' He laughed and sent the skittish horse skipping away across the plaza. He jumped down outside Aristide's, gave a wave and went inside.

'It's not fair,' Ruth murmured, touching fingers to her lips with a kind of awe, wanting to treasure the kiss for a few seconds. 'Why can't he take me with him?'

Then she straightened her hair and dress. 'No, I guess that's impossible.' And she went back to join the others in their disapproving silence.

# 6

The soldiers' bugle calling reveille woke *El Borracho*, who, with his two companions, was sprawled out in a corner of the colonnade. He unwrapped his *serape* from around his huge body and groaned. He had hit the tequila hard the night before. Not unusual. It was the first light of dawn and in the middle of the plaza Almedo's muleteers were stirring. They, too, had spent the night under the stars as was their custom.

The big Mexican clambered to his feet, saddled his mustang and, accompanied by Gustavo and Miguel, lumbered across to cadge a mug of coffee. The muleteers had a brazier burning and their pot bubbling. It smelt good and tasted better, scalding the stale taste of alcohol from their throats and warming their bellies.

'First thing I'm gonna do,' *El Borracho*

growled, 'is take a look at where that blonde sweetheart's got to.'

Gustavo demurred. 'Didn't we oughta wait see what the *gringo*, Williams, says?'

'I don't take orders from that lily-livered one.' *El Borracho* scratched at his lice-infested vest and grinned. 'He can sort out the ransom on the two girls. They're small-fry. We got bigger fish to catch. This dish will be worth a fortune back in Old Mexico, even after we've had our way with her.'

Miguel flashed his teeth lecherously, but also looked a tad worried. 'What about Espinosa?'

'What about him? He doesn't own us. I'm sick of him getting all the cash, the pick of the women. We'll grab that honey and get out.'

★　★　★

Ruth Simms had spent a cramped night sleeping in a bed with the three girls, listening to the whine and whistle of her uncle's snores from the next room. At

78

least, she thought, she was snug and safe here after the nightmare of the past days.

The house was bustling as her uncle opened the store, the girls swept and tidied and their mother made a sparse breakfast. 'Where's the privy?' Ruth asked.

'Down the bottom of the yard.' Her aunt pointed. 'Hurry. There's plenty to do. Mr Simms likes to keep us busy.'

'I bet he does,' Ruth murmured.

When she stepped from the three-seater privy and straightened her dress the girl looked up at the blue sky. It was going to be another fine day. She did not fancy spending it in the store. But, she guessed, needs must.

Suddenly she heard a step behind her and a filthy hand closed over her mouth, gagging her as she struggled and tried to scream out. A huge man closed his arms tight around her and dragged her back through the yard gate. She could smell his foul breath and sweat. 'Oh, no!' she moaned through his fingers.

'Got her!' *El Borracho* exclaimed, slipping a rawhide noose over her head and tightening it around her throat. 'Hold still, you wildcat.' He twisted her arms behind her back and wound the rope tight around her wrists. He slammed her up against the fence and tore her cotton dress open to reveal her white breasts.

'What a beauty, huh?' He gave a hoarse chuckle, tempted to take her then and there.

'C'mon, *amigo*.' Miguel whirled his mustang. 'We got to ride.'

'Sure.' *El Borracho* gripped Ruth by the hair and grinned broken teeth at her. 'We got plenty time.' When Ruth gave a shrill scream he crashed his fist across her jaw, almost knocking her senseless. 'Shut up, you bitch. That's just a taster.'

The big man caught a hand under her bare thigh to sling her, legs apart, over the front of Miguel's saddle. 'Here, you take her. You don't weigh much.'

Indeed, his own mustang had enough

to do carrying him. He clambered into the saddle and slashed its hindquarters with the knotted quirt on his wrist. '*Hola!*' he sang out. '*Arriba!*'

As the three horsemen set off away from the town all Ruth could do was give a shrill cry of, 'Help me!' But it seemed a faint hope.

Seth Tobin, after a late night at the casino, had bedded down in the livery with Star and was tying his blanket roll preparing to leave when he heard the faint cry.

'Shee-it!' He looked across the rocky terrain and saw the Mexicans disappearing at full gallop in a cloud of dust. And he had glimpsed the flow of the girl's golden hair glinting in the morning sunlight. 'What's happening?'

That, he guessed, was pretty evident. He had no time to raise the alarm. He snatched up his Sharps and vaulted into the saddle, swirling the stallion around and haring after them. They appeared to be heading south for some reason, towards Santa Fe.

The stallion's hoofs were drumming the hard ground, his mane blowing in the wind, as Seth urged him on, long pale tail trailing out behind him as he swerved to avoid rocks and pitfalls.

The frontiersman raised the Sharps tight to his shoulder and snapped out a shot but the riders were too far off and it only made them gallop harder. It crossed Seth's mind they might haul in among the bigger rocks and wait in ambush. Three desperate men against one was not good odds.

He galloped on across the plateau through the wind-eroded rocks of all shapes and sizes. His powerful stallion was slowly gaining on them, but how long could he keep going at that speed? It occurred to Seth that if they followed the curving trail they were following there was a short-cut he could take across the hills. It was a gamble, but a cry from the girl made up his mind for him.

The youngster swerved his mount to the right and headed him leaping up the side of a hill. It was a hard struggle but they made it to the top. He whirled Star around to see where his quarry was and pricked spurs to the stallion's sides sending him ploughing down through steep shale. At the foot of the slope he charged off once more. When he reached his destination he inserted another cartridge in the Sharps.

Miguel had one lean arm around the girl as he rode, glancing back to see where their pursuer had got to. As he did so Seth Tobin leaped from a rock overhang, flying through the air to knock both him and his captive rolling and crashing from the mustang.

It was a hard landing, knocking the breath from Miguel's body as the horse went tumbling too. The wiry Mexican looked up with alarm, struggling to find his rifle, but the American was on his feet first. His revolver barked flame and Miguel screamed as the .38 slug ploughed bloodily through his chest.

'One down,' Seth gritted out, glancing at the girl who was lying prone. 'Two to go.'

Gustavo had spun his horse around and with Mexican fatalism was charging back towards him and had already started foolishly blamming away with his six-gun. Seth held the Paterson at arm's length, faced the flying lead and, waiting his chance, fired three times. Blood spurted from Gustavo's forehead and he tumbled from the saddle to lie dead, eyes staring, at Seth's feet.

One bullet left.

*El Borracho* had reined in and started back towards them, but seeing his two *compadres* on the ground he hesitated. He was seventy paces away. Too far for his Volcanic to be accurate.

Seth put fingers to his lips and gave a piercing whistle. His pale, finely muscled stallion came trotting around from the back of the rocks, tossing his head, and approached obediently. The long-legged American ran to pull his Sharps from the saddle cinch. One bullet ready in that, too.

Seth bit his lip anxiously, resting the Sharp's long barrel on the stallion's saddle as *El Borracho*'s shots whined past him. He squeezed the trigger and saw a look of alarm spread over the giant Mexican's ugly face as he clutched at his shoulder and blood oozed through his fingers.

*El Borracho* didn't wait to do further battle, but, cursing and vowing vengeance, hauled his mustang around and, lashing it cruelly, raced for his life.

Seth tossed the Sharps aside, swung into the saddle and charged after him, but when he reached the end of the high rocks saw the Mexican in the distance, kicking up a spiral of dust, heading back north.

'Damn you,' Tobin muttered, and went back to the fallen girl.

He jumped down to kneel beside her, patting her cheek, hardly able to restrain a lick of sexual desire as he saw her bare breasts, their pert, pink-tipped nipples. 'Come on,' he said. 'Are you OK?'

Ruth opened her eyelids and stared at him with a kind of helplessness.

'Seth,' she murmured. 'Where did you spring from?'

'Them good looks of yourn certainly git a gal in trouble,' he drawled with a grin. 'But I can see why.'

'Goodness!' she exclaimed, following his gaze. 'Look at me!'

'Yeah, I *was* doing.'

She hastily tried to pull together her torn dress. Blood was trickling from her lip.

'I said are you OK?'

She touched her jaw and waggled it. 'Yes, I think so. The big brute gave me such a clonk. Where is he?'

'He got away.' He helped her to her feet and on to one of the dead Mexican's mustangs. Then he regained his own saddle and caught the reins of the other horse. 'I guess I kin hang on to the horses. Seems the only repayment I'll get for my efforts.'

She looked across at him, stroking the hair from her eyes. 'What do you expect?'

Seth shrugged and kneed the stallion

away. 'C'mon. I'm s'posed to be headin'
for Cañon City, not Santa Fe.'

*   *   *

Before they got back to town, however,
they were met by George Ravilious, in
his plumed campaign hat, and the more
sombre Captain Reynolds, his infantry
commander, who were riding 'to the
rescue'. And a bunch of excited
storekeepers, their wives and children,
were waiting for them when they
arrived in Taos, loudly demanding
action by the army against the scandal-
ous depradations of the Mexicans.

Ravilious rode in beside Ruth,
handing her down from her horse and
giving the impression that he was
responsible for her safety as he escorted
her into the Simms household.

Ezekiel Simms demanded that a
public meeting be held in the gospel
hall immediately and Captain Ravilious
airily replied, 'By all means. I'm
prepared to answer any question you

care to fire at me.'

'Why ain't you brought the cavalry?' the town blacksmith demanded, when folks had settled themselves in the hall. 'What good is infantry in chasin' Indians and Mexican bandits? They're away to the hills before you even git started.'

'My dear fellow, don't underestimate the infantry.' Ravilious adopted a defiant stance in the pulpit of the hall. 'Our information is that the savages who committed the massacre at Pueblo have returned to the San Juan range. We intend to send a punitive expedition against them. I doubt if they'll like a taste of our guns. But first I will seek out and attack Espinosa in his hideout. You may rest assured we will rid you of this bandit once and for all.'

There was a caustic howl of incredulity at this. 'Aw, we've heard that all before,' Ezekiel Simms cried. 'What you gonna do in the meantime to protect our wimmin and girls?'

'I suggest you form your own

voluntary brigade to protect the town in times of emergency,' the captain replied. 'Arm yourselves and be in readiness.'

'We ain't gunfighters,' Ezekiel protested. 'We're traders. What chance we got against them devils?'

Ravilious went on the defensive, explaining that the frontier forts were few and far between, undermanned, ill-provided, lacking experienced officers, doing their best with untrained recruits. 'Do you realize I am allowed only six rounds of ammunition per week a man for target practice? I can hardly turn them into dead-shots.'

Señor Almedo had been listening and spoke out. 'Before you go turning your howitzers on Espinosa's hideout, should you ever find it, I suggest you proceed with caution. Young Miss Simms has had a very lucky escape this morning, but I should remind you I have been informed he is holding my two young nieces and demanding a ransom. I am most concerned no harm befalls them.'

'That's right,' Hal Williams butted in,

worried he might lose his cut of the ransom. 'I'm pretty sure I can lead you to him and arrange the handover.'

'Durn Mexicans,' a woman sang out. 'They're the cause of this trouble. Oughta be shot on sight.'

'Please, no need for remarks like that,' the captain cautioned. 'Law-abiding Mexicans have as much right to army protection now as all other Americans.'

'In that case,' the settler woman spat out, 'why doncha git on with pertectin' us 'stead of spoutin' all this balloon juice?'

'Why don't you elect yourselves a law officer to be paid out of town funds?' Captain Reynolds grunted, breaking his customary silence. 'Then he could organize a posse when needs be.'

'Yep, that's not a bad idea,' the blacksmith agreed. 'We obviously cain't rely on the overstretched army. How about you, Mr Carson? Would you be ready to stand?'

All eyes turned to a colourful figure

standing to one side, an American, in a flamboyant curved-brim hat, frock coat, bandanna, and chaps of buckskin pinned at their edges by silver conchos. He was in his forties, grey-tinged hair hanging to his shoulders, regular of features, with a solid lantern jaw. Christopher 'Kit' Carson was a renowned frontiersman, famed for guiding Fremont and his government expedition through the Rockies. He had married a Mexican girl and was a resident of Taos.

'I don't think you could afford me,' he said, with a smile. 'I'm a businessman and time, as you know, is money. How about you, Seth, my friend? You're pretty handy with a gun. You blew out the candle for two of Espinosa's thugs today, I hear. It was quick thinking. And you know this country like the back of your hand.'

It was Seth's turn to prevaricate. He tipped his hat over his brow and scratched the back of his head with embarrassment. 'Waal, you see, I'm like you, I'm pretty busy right now. I'm on the point of going into business on my own.'

He had worked for Carson four years before when he had been seventeen, helping drive a flock of 6,500 sheep from Taos to the California goldfields, a feat never tried before. Carson had made a nice profit, but as his employee Seth had received a token fifty dollars. Another reason why he planned to set up on his own.

'Of course, in emergency, if I'm around, I'm allus ready to lend a hand, as you know, but' — he thought he might as well throw in a free advertisement — 'in the meantime I'll be haulin' freight 'tween here and the mines in Cañon City.'

Kit Carson grinned. 'Sounds like the sheriff's job wouldn't pay enough for you, either. Look here, Cap, 'fore you go tweakin' Espinosa's tail maybe we better git Señor Almedo's nieces out alive first. If there's a ransom involved I'm willing to go along with Williams and negotiate. Then you can start blastin' your howitzer and catch 'em if you can.'

When the meeting broke up, without much having been decided, Seth was persuaded to go along to Aristide's casino for a drink with Carson, Almedo and Ravilious.

As the whiskey was passed around Kit remarked, 'So, you've decided to become an entrepreneur, Seth? I should warn you it ain't all honey.'

'That's what I've told him,' Almedo put in. 'He's turned down a well-paid offer to be my wagonmaster.'

'Waal, this is a wide-open country, gents, with big prospects for settlement.' Seth raised his glass to them. 'So I've decided to follow your example and scoop off some of the cream. At least, that's my aim.'

Carson gave a hearty guffaw. 'She sure was a beauty of a blonde charmer you rescued from a fate worse than death, Seth. If I were you I'd saddle up that filly purty fast or she might not be available when you git back. Git my meaning? You want to watch out for Alfredo here. He's been widowed a year and I bet he's on the qui vive for a new bed-warmer.'

For the first time in his life a jolt of jealousy hit Seth as he scowled at the Mexican trader. 'She'll wait,' he whispered. 'She ain't the type to take up with a rich old daddy.'

'Don't be too sure about that.' Carson winked at the captain. 'You don't think she'll want to be skivvy for that skinflint Bible-basher Ezekiel Simms for long, do you?'

'All's fair in love and war.' Almedo smiled and tossed back his silver hair. 'I may well present my compliments to the young lady.'

Carson laughed, harshly. 'An' I figure the captain here wouldn't be averse to gittin' his hands into her calico drawers, either. Of course, she ain't of his social register so I doubt if he'd be offerin' marriage.'

'You put it so crudely,' Ravilious replied,

'but, yes, Miss Simms has rather taken my fancy.'

'You keep your hands offen her, you dirty old lechers,' Seth growled, getting to his feet and reaching for his Sharps. 'Or you'll have me to contend with. Thanks for the drink, Kit. I gotta be going.'

Carson chuckled as he watched him go. 'Now you've really got the young rooster riled-up, gents. I thought for a moment he was going to take a swing at either or both of you.'

# 7

The 4,000-foot snow-crested peaks of the Sangre de Cristo range, the haunt of Espinosa and his blood-thirsty crew, stretched away to the east, while the pine-girt mass of the San Juans, where hostile Utes lurked, lay to the west as Seth Tobin made his way north along the Rio Grande. He urged his high-stepping stallion on, snapping his rope-end at the two saddle horses of the dead *bandidos*, which he figured might come in handy, sending them cantering before him.

Before night fell he loose-hitched them. With quick economy he axed pine boughs to erect a half-bivouac against the mountain gusts, got out his line and flies and quickly caught three speckled trout from the sparkling river. In next to no time he had supper frying over his small fire, burnt the remains so as not to attract bears, and took a pull on a bottle of dago red.

He settled back in his water-proofed, feather-filled bag against his saddle and watched the setting sun flushing the mountain peaks in a crimson glow. Little wonder the Spanish conquistadors had named this area Colorado.

As the night deepened the sky took on an indigo clarity, the moon rising and stars flashing as thick as confetti in the space out yonder. The pinprick red glow of the planet Mars, Sirius the dog star, and the other constellations was clearly visible in the mountain air. After a decade of wandering, sleeping outside never bothered him. It was bunking indoors that took some getting used to, but was, of course, welcome when the blizzards set in.

He tucked his revolver under the saddle, stuck his knife in the sand, tossed more wood on the fire and shoved the Sharps down between his knees. It was not only Indians, Mexicans and white desperados he had to be wary of, but grizzlies, cougars on the prowl, and other various varmints, too. But the wine and the fifty-mile ride soon took their effect. He woke with the dawn to the sound of the rushing stream and the horses cropping the flower-strewn grass. Time to journey on.

When he passed the small town of Alamosa, Seth headed on, casting off from the Rio Grande valley and skirting the western edge of the great sand-dune desert. He had another eighty miles to go to Cañon City, but reached the upper Arkansas River without incident, or, indeed, sight of another human. In the distance, Pike's Peak reared up amid the saw-toothed ranges. Yet to be accurately measured, it was estimated at 15,000 feet high. In fact, this southern area of the Rockies was barely mapped and described, when it was, as 'unorganized territory'.

Those who roamed it, apart from the Utes, were mainly mountain men, trappers and prospectors. There had been some small finds in the Pike's Peak area but the miners had yet to hit it big. Gold was being taken out around Cañon City, which was why the ramshackle town had sprung up. But nothing to attract a stampede.

Seth himself had never had much luck gold-panning. He had given it a go at Sacramento but it had proved back-breaking work with, in his case, little gain. He had decided there was more money to be made supplying the miners' needs.

When he trotted his stallion into the so-called 'city' he was expecting his future partner, Jack Jackson, to have bought wagons and mules with the cash he had forwarded him and be ready to start operating. How wrong could he be?

Like its name implied, Cañon City was built beneath the walls of a canyon that hung over it on both sides of the infant, but fast-flowing Arkansas stream. Some miles further east the river, over the millenia, had cut a huge, precipitous gorge through which it thundered, almost impassable to man. Then it wound its way more leisurely across the great plains until it reached the Mississippi.

The township was a jumbled array of cabins and lean-tos against the cliff, a variety of stores, and false-fronted saloons where the flotsam which such places attracted tried to skin the miners of their hard-won gains. The main trail was littered with half-sawn timber, piles of rubbish and waste. Outside The Crimson Garter lay the bloated corpse of a mule at which ravens pecked.

In various gulches nearby numerous grubby individuals hacked away at mine shafts convinced they were about to hit it big. So far this had proved an illusion. Cañon City was by no means a boom town.

'Seen Jack Jackson?' Seth enquired of an old guy who was sitting on the sidewalk watching him hitch his horses.

The gent squinted at him and jerked a thumb back at The Crimson Garter. 'He ain't put the stopper in the bottle in a 'coon's age,' he crooned. 'Since Lulu slung her hook.'

'You don't say.' Seth stepped up on to the sidewalk and pushed into the saloon. Jack was a sight for sore eyes, sprawled over the bar in a filthy undervest, his trousers suspended by bits of string, his face as grey as his mussed hair as he stared with rheumy red eyes at an almost empty bottle in his hand.

'Hey, I thought we were going into business,' Tobin said. 'What's going on? Did you use the cash I gave ya to buy them mules?'

'She's gawn. The greatest li'l gal in the whole wide world.' Jackson clawed at Seth's shirt, pleading, 'Why did she do it, pardner?'

'Because you're a pathetic, feckless idiot, I should think. Pull yourself together, Jack, the whole town's laughing at you. Your reputation's lower than a rattler's belly.'

'Why did she walk out on me, Seth?' Jackson moaned. 'What did I do wrong?'

The barkeep, a man as bald as a billiard ball, with a massive moustache to compensate, was polishing glasses and grinned widely. 'So it's your money he's been spending? Have a beer on the house, pal. Then git your partner outa here. I've had enough of him.'

'How much of my capital you got left, Jack?' Seth grabbed him, threateningly, by his vest. 'Hand it over 'fore it's all gawn.'

'What? I dunno.' Jackson tipped the last drops of whiskey from the bottle. He desperately emptied the tumbler down his throat and fumbled in his pockets to find cash. Amid assorted rubbish all he produced was a few cents. 'There y'are. Don't worry, pal, I'll pay you back.'

A past-her-prime prostitute, a dumpy woman in a stained taffeta dress and red stockings, was sprawled on a battered sofa nearby. 'What's so special about Lulu?' she sang out. 'She's just a whore like us all.'

'Lulu was boot-ee-fool,' Jack slurred,

waving his arms as if to indicate her curves. 'I love that gal. Where you reckon she's gone, Seth?'

'As far away from you as possible, I should think.' The young frontiersman raised the glass mug of beer slid along to him. 'I'm sorry, Jack. You ain't a partner of mine no more. I'm terminatin' our agreement. I need to make money and you ain't gonna help me none.'

'Hey, don't be like that, Seth,' Jackson whined, grabbing at his arm. 'Just buy me another drink. I'll be fine in the mornin'.'

'He's as nutty as squirrel shit!' The whore's chubby face glistened with sweat beneath paint and rouge. With vain affectation she stroked back her thinning, hennaed hair. 'Hey, mister, you lookin' for a real woman?' She coyly raised her dress to reveal her pudgy thighs. 'How about it?'

Seth slapped a silver dollar on the bartop. 'Give him another bottle,' he said. 'And a drink for Rancid Rita. I'm outa here.'

Outside in the street he gathered his reins and leaned on Star's saddle considering his predicament. 'Jeesis Christ! How can a man git so besotted over a woman like that? He must be crazy. Come on, let's git outa this stinkin' hole.'

Suddenly a reedy voice with a Scots twang sang out, 'Ye look like a man who's lost a dollar and found a dime.'

Seth spun around and saw a gnarled back-woodsman sporting a tam o'shanter, a buckskin breastplate, bony knees poking from a heavy tartan kilt, a dirk in one of his thick woollen socks, a cutlass on his belt and an ancient longarm in his grip.

'Dick McGhee!' he laughed. 'You ol' buzzard. I thought you were dead.'

In spite of his appearance McGhee was a legendary figure in Colorado. A crack shot, he was renowned for his ability to kill two antelope with one shot from his Hawken rifle.

'Ach! They won't bury me in a hurry.' The Scotsman put a strong, wiry arm around the youngster. 'Good to see you, Seth. What are ye up to in this place?'

'It's a long story. I'd buy you a drink, old-timer, but not in there.' He nodded at The Crimson Garter. 'Where's another watering-hole?'

'For you, nothing but the best, my son. I've a barrel of moonshine, brewed it myself. Ye'll be comin' hame with me.' Not waiting for a reply he led the way on foot out of town and turned up into the wooded canyonside until he reached a mineshaft and cabin. 'Come on in and meet Josepha. I expect that damn Frenchie's here trying to cosy up to her.'

There were pelts pegged out on the cabin front and antlers scattered about amid mining debris. Inside, a tin stove was burning and a middle-aged, grey-haired Mexican woman was stirring a cauldron.

'Look who's here,' McGhee cried, 'my old friend, Seth Tobin. You've heard me yarn about him. He was a barefoot, ragged, thirteen-year-old when I took him under my wing in Taos. Now behold the strapping young fellow.'

'They were good days, Dick.'

Indeed, after both his mother and father had died of the fever at their small farm in Missouri and Seth had set off across the plains, 'Uncle Dick' had semi-adopted him, taught him all he knew as they roamed the Rockies, working as guides and trappers.

The other occupant of the cabin was a surly Frenchman, in a red wool cap, sitting on a stool whittling at a stick. The Scotsman ignored him as he fetched his small barrel of whiskey, took a cutglass tumbler from his sporran, filled it to the brim from the spigot and announced, 'Ye're the favoured son. You get the loan of my very own glass.'

Seth sampled the brew tentatively. One swallow sent shockwaves through his system. 'You ain't lost your touch, Dick. I'm gonna have to take it easy with this.'

'Och, mon, get it doon.' Dick filled a

clay mug for himself and ignored the beseeching look of Pierre. 'It's too good for a Froggie,' he said. 'Git to the town if you want to drink. What you doin' in here, anyway, soon as my back's turned, as if I didn't know?'

'*M'sieu*,' Pierre protested. 'You got me all wrong.'

Seth explained his business in Cañon City, how it had gone wrong, and found himself telling them about his meeting with Ruth Simms and how he needed to make some cash if he were to have any chance with that gal. The whiskey must have loosened his tongue.

'No decent girl wan' to get meex up with some down-at-heel prairie rat,' Pierre put in. 'You got no chance.'

'Not if that old dog Almedo's sniffing around,' McGhee agreed. 'You shoulda grabbed her an' brought her up here. Who the hell bothers with the benefit of clergy in these parts?'

Josepha, who was bustling about, frowned. 'If she's a decent girl she wan' a good home and a gold ring on her finger.' She displayed her own which was significantly bare.

'I jest cain't understand folks allus hankering to git wed,' the Scotsman protested. 'The unholiest institution ever invented. A recipe for strife and disaster. Take my advice, boy, avoid it like the plague.'

'It ain't like that.' Seth shook his head and stared at the stove. 'This is the real thang. I'm fair taken with her, Dick. That rat, Jack Jackson, might have boozed away all my cash, but I guess, in a way, I'm bitten by the same affliction as him.'

'You follow your head and your heart,' Josepha advised as she dished out a gamey 'sonuvabitch stew', bits and pieces of just about everything flavoured with red hot chillis. 'But drinkin' that firewater don't help nobody.'

When they had filled their bellies McGhee pushed back his chair and reminisced about the big journey they had made back in '42, a 5,000-mile trip from Fort Bent on the River Arkansas up through the Rockies, then on to the Big Horns and the wondrous Yellowstone plateau. They had explored the Snake and Big Salmon rivers and lived with the Shoshoni, friendly to the whites in those days before they learned better.

'Yeah,' Seth sighed. 'Their land was like an untouched paradise. How long were we there, Dick? I coulda stayed there forever.'

'Almost a year. Remember old chief Spotted Wolf?'

'Yep. He wanted to marry his daughters to me, not one but the whole durn six.'

'You shoulda taken him up on it, boy, instead of poachin' one of 'em. It was on account of you we had to git outa there fast.'

'No,' Seth disagreed. 'You *made* me leave.'

'I had to look after your interests. You were only fourteen. Whose side is it best to be on? The Injins' or the white man's. We started out with nineteen men and we'd already had five killed by Piutes. I didn't want to lose no more.'

'Where you go,' Pierre growled, 'from the Snake?'

'Aye, we marched down through Oregon to San Luis Obispo, California. Headed south, reached the Gila River and back east to Fort Bent. By God, they were surprised to see us. We'd been away two whole years.'

'The trip of a lifetime,' Seth mused. 'I started out a boy but I guess by the time I got back I was a man.'

'We were loaded with beaver packs dried out hard as boards on our ponies. I made five thousand dollars selling our peltry back in the states. One beaver was fetching fifteen dollars, an amazing price. You wouldn't get a plug of baccy for one today.'

Seth took a sup of the coffee Josepha poured. 'I can't say I liked all the trapping and killing. Them poor critters didn't harm nobody, just busy building their lodges and swimming about. They were practically wiped out.'

'They'll make a comeback,' McGhee roared, in his aggressive way. 'Ye're as soft as a gal sometimes, Seth. Anyway the bottom's dropped out of the beaver trade. Fashions have changed. Gents back East and Europe don't wear beaver hats no more. They've taken to silk toppers, instead.'

'Waal, I wanted to make a living some other way. That's why I got out. But I'm surprised you've given up trapping, Dick. Never thought you'd turn gold miner.'

'He don' work the mine,' Pierre snarled. 'It's me does all the diggin' and hard work.'

'So?' the Scotsman shouted. 'I own it. You're just me employee, you snivellin' Frenchie. Ye're so damn idle we barely make a handful of dollars a week from it.'

He winked at Seth and poured some more whiskey from the barrel. 'No, I don't do much trapping these days, but I've been buying pelts and quilled robes from the Utes. I got a stack of them in the mine. I was going to take them down to Bent's Fort, but I heard it got burned to the ground.'

'True,' Seth replied. 'You could see the flames from fifty miles away. Some say drunken Arapahoes set light to the powder store while Bill Bent was away at Big Timbers visiting the Cheyenne.'

'Rubbish, mon!' McGhee cried. 'In my opinion the ornery ol' 'breed blew it sky-high himself. He'd been trying to sell the fort to the US Government but they wouldn't pay his price.'

'Wouldn't put it past him.' Seth recalled the famous outpost on the plains, with its twenty-feet high adobe walls and fortified martellos. It had contained huge stores, wagon sheds, smithies, saddlers' and carpenters' shops. It would teem with travellers, traders, Mexicans, Indians, for the Bent brothers had married into the Cheyenne. Once a year, mountain men and French *voyageurs* would descend upon it for a riotous, drunken jamboree as they sold their pelts. 'What a hullabaloo there used to be.'

'Those days are all but over now.' McGhee looked gloomily at his whiskey. 'We won't see the like of it agin.'

'Why,' Seth suggested, 'don't you take your pelts down to Santa Fe and sell them?'

'Och, I'm too old to be botherin'. I've hid a pot of gold coins up in the hills for me old age. Trouble is,' he added cannily, glancing at Josepha, 'I can't recall where I hid it.'

'In that case why don't I take them to Taos and Santa Fe for you and give you a fair price when I git back?'

'Why not? Come to think of it there's an old beat-up wagon at the back of the blacksmith's. Why don't you do it up an' you'll be in business, boy.'

'Yes,' Seth mused, 'the Tobin Teamster Company. How does that sound?'

'Well, one wagon don't match yon Spaniard's twenty-three, nor his hundred and fifty bulls and uncountable horses. But it's a start. Sounds good,

Seth. Old Alfredo had better watch out!'

★ ★ ★

Since President 'Old Hickory' Jackson's ruckus with the banks he had made sure there was a good supply of gold coins minted. Men had become shy of paper money. Its one benefit was easy portability. Luckily Seth had been paid by Señor Almedo in $20 cartwheels for there was no way Dick McGhee would accept notes.

In the morning he proudly showed Seth his stash of pelts — 'coon skins, fox furs, marten, mink and supple buckskins which Indian squaws softened by chewing with their teeth. 'These'll readily sell for a thousand dollars in Santa Fe.'

'I ain't got nuthin' like that. I'd have to owe ya.'

'Give me what you got, laddie' — McGhee spoke in an odd mixture of broad Scots and mountain man drawl

— 'don't hold back.'

Seth fished out his four gold coins. 'Eighty dollars. That's my lot.'

'Done.' McGhee took the gold and clasped his hand. 'You don't owe me nuthin'. Regard it as a gift. Och, I ain't got nobody else in the world. Ye're like a son to me. I'm glad to be able to set ye up. Besides they didn't cost me much.'

Seth studied a nicely quilled robe. 'You got this from the Utes?'

'Where else? They know better than to give me grief. They wouldn't get any more bullets, would they?'

'Ain't that against the law? Selling arms to the Indians.'

'If so you better keep it under your hat. Yon mountain cat cost me a pound of powder, guncaps and sixty balls. Them ancient flintlock *fusées* they got might have a bore as big as a wee cannon but they ain't likely to bother the army much.'

'How about these buckskins?'

'I believe that cost me a butcher's

knife. They'll trade for a few charges of powder or even a bead necklace. You know how fond they are of them gimcracks.'

'But that business down at Pueblo, don't it bother you?'

'Och, someone or something got 'em mad. The medicine men get 'em all stirred up and before you know it the young bucks are racing off down to the plain looking for scalps. Them folks in the pueblo shouldn't have opened the gates to 'em. Surely they saw they was wearin' paint?'

'Men, wimmin, kids — only one survivor, Dick.'

'What's done's done. You know what they're like. A sudden surge of blood-lust then they simmer down, carry on as if nothing has occurred.'

'That jackanapes Captain Ravilious is planning to punish them.'

'He'd be a fool if he does. Just stir up more trouble. C'mon, finish up your oatcakes. Let's go take a look at that wagon.'

On the way McGhee collared a runaway slave, and took him along. 'Clarence here's the best carpenter in town. He owes me for whiskey. He'll soon have yon wagon fixed up.'

The derelict wagon cost the young frontiersman his last five dollars and he gave it a lick of paint himself while Clarence worked. He carefully enscrolled 'Tobin Teamsters' on the side and the next day, the two spare horses in the shafts, Star trotting along behind, and well loaded, he moved out. 'Giddap!' he shouted as McGhee waved farewell. 'We're in business, boys. We're on our way.'

# 8

'You cowardly son of a whore,' Espinosa screamed, as *El Borracho* swung back and forth over a fierce fire tied by his heels to the jutting branch of a pine. 'You yellow-livered pisspot! I'll teach you! You dare to crawl back here and tell me two of my best men are dead?'

'Ow!' El Borracho howled, as his ears singed. He tried to hunch himself up to avoid the flames but it was not easy with his wrists bound behind his back. 'There was nothing I could do, I swear. I fought like a lion but there must have been twenty *Americanos*. I was lucky to escape with my life.'

His comrades cackled at the frantic look on the buffoon's face as they swung him back and forth. 'Look at him wriggle,' one sniggered, 'like a fat worm on a hook.'

'*Sí.*' Espinosa sent his bullwhip snaking to lash across *El Borracho's* chest. 'A fat piece of offal more like.'

'No, *jefe!*' the big man begged in between screams as the whip found its mark. Why had he come back? When Espinosa got into a rage there was no knowing what he would do. 'I risked their gunfire to get a prize for you. Ow!'

'A prize? What prize?' Espinosa strode forward and lashed him again. 'Don't you dare lie to me, squitface.'

'A girl. Such a girl!' *El Borracho* shrieked. 'I had her in my arms but he, the *Americano*, stopped me. I mean *they* did.'

'Liar! So that's it. Three of you couldn't deal with one *gringo*. Ach, cut him down. I might as well make cabbage soup of his head as try to talk any sense into it.'

*El Borracho* landed with a thump in the fire and scrambled out, flapping at his smouldering hair and garments. Whimpering, he crawled away. 'It is not fair. You have never seen such a beauty.'

'What?' In spite of his anger Espinosa was interested. 'Don't you lie to me again.'

'I would never lie to you, *jefe*. I tell you I had her in my arms. Such pink-tipped breasts of whitest snow. Such golden hair. Such eyes as blue as the skies. And to have her plucked from me.'

'You lying pig!' Espinosa frowned and cracked the whip at him again. 'There is no such woman hereabouts.'

*El Borracho* backed away. 'No, *señor*, perhaps I was mistaken. Perhaps the sun spun my head. Perhaps there was no such girl. *Sí*, perhaps she was an ugly old hag.'

'Oh, shut up, you ape.' Espinosa gave him a last hissing snap of the whip. 'Why do I surround myself with cretins?'

He went to sit on his saddle draped over a rock, pushed fingers through his thick black curls. What if there was such a prize?

'Pedro,' he shouted to another of his

men. 'You are little known in Taos. Go there, speak to my sister and the *gringo*, Williams, find out when they will bring the gold for these two useless girls. Tell the trader Almedo that if the cash is not here by the third day from now they will have their throats slit.'

'*Sí, jefe.*' The lithe Mexican ran to leap on his mustang, brandished his rifle. 'I will be back as soon as I know.'

'Wait!' Espinosa hollered. 'Not so fast. Find out if there is such a woman as this golden-haired American girl. If so, we will have her.'

He turned to *El Borracho* as Pedro went cantering away down the mountainside. 'If you speak the truth I will reward you. If you *have* lied to me, I will kill you.'

★ ★ ★

Señor Alfredo Almedo had not been slow to get his knees under the table at the Simms's house, so to speak. He had called to enquire about Ruth's health the day after her attempted kidnapping, presenting her with a large bouquet of flowers and inviting her to take a drive in his landau.

'I don't see why not,' Ezekiel squawked. 'I can spare her from her duties for an hour or so. Of course, my wife will have to go with you as chaperon.'

It had occurred to the crafty shopkeeper that he might be able to squeeze some cash out of the wealthy Spaniard if he was serious about marrying the girl. Usually a dowry came with a woman, but he had in mind a reverse one of, say, $2,000 in gold payable to him. 'If he wants the young hussy as his bride he'll have to pay,' he muttered.

The silver-haired hidalgo sat very formally in the Simms's parlour as refreshments were served, his sombrero on his lap. But as soon as Mrs Simms went out to the kitchen he was down on one knee, clutching at Ruth's hands to kiss them, gazing up at her with dark and languorous eyes, begging her to have pity for his tormented passion.

The amorous old goat quickly, if rather arthritically, got back on his chair when Mrs Simms returned in her best shawl and sunbonnet. 'Ah, are we ready for the outing?' he cried. 'How splendid.'

At least it was pleasant to get away from the oppressive atmosphere of the store as the landau and its pair of matching greys went jogging away out of town. Almedo, on the opposite seat to the two ladies, raised a hand to acknowledge acquaintances as they passed, and Ruth, with her parasol for protection from the sun, felt rather like the pictures she had seen of European royalty.

'One day I will take you out to my ranch,' Alfredo smiled. 'My youngest son runs it for me. His brother is a lawyer in Santa Fe.'

Just as well he was for many *dons* had been swindled out of their land rights when they became part of the

USA. His son had made sure their vast ranch, which had been the possession of the Almedo family for generations, was legally protected.

Alfredo sat back and admired the girl's exquisite face and hair, the ample bosom and lithe thighs which even the dowdy, worn, ankle-length dress the Simmses had provided could not disguise. Mentally he was wondering how he could lure her back to his town house on his own one evening. Somehow he would have to get rid of the tiresome Mildred.

'Such a gentleman,' Mildred sighed, after he returned them to the store. 'What a catch he would be for you.'

Ruth made a downturned grimace, shuddering at the prospect of being bed companion to the middle-aged Spaniard. 'He seems pleasant enough,' she replied, 'but if I'm allowed any say in the matter I would prefer a man more of my own age.'

And now Captain Ravilious was hanging around the store waiting for her, clicking his heels, attempting to kiss her hand, asking if she might care to attend the dance at the casino with him on the occasion of the forthcoming fiesta.

'That certainly sounds like more fun than Señor Almedo has in mind,' Ruth smiled, but Ezekiel quickly stepped in and forbade her.

'Out of the question, Captain,' he shouted, indignantly. 'Mine is a God-fearing family. We will have no truck with dancing, drinking and the Roman Catholic worship of painted statues. Fiesta, indeed! It is just an excuse to down tools and engage in debauchery.'

'At least he's in his thirties and a Protestant,' Mildred remarked when Ravilious had gone. 'A captain's wage isn't to be sniffed at, Ruth. You *are* the lucky one.'

'You think so?' Ruth said. 'Personally I'm not sure the captain's attentions or intentions are completely honourable.'

★ ★ ★

Almedo had returned to his spacious town house, formerly a bishop's palace when Taos was part of the farflung Mexican empire. The street frontage was barred and fortified, but inside the numerous rooms were set around a courtyard, a veritable oasis of fountains, ferns, plants and pool, cool and shady to sit around. There was a banqueting chamber, a private chapel, huge religious oil paintings on the walls, blue and white tiled floors, and generally an air of luxury.

He was not a little surprised to find that the gambler, Hal Williams, and Espinosa's sister, Teresa, had called and were waiting for him. But he made a shrewd guess at what they were after. 'No doubt you've come about a ransom for my nieces,' he snapped. 'So, how much does that brigand want?'

'We saw your nieces,' Teresa cried. 'The poor creatures are terrified. Although unharmed as yet I dread to think what might happen to them. You must help them.'

'Must I? Who are you, some singer in a bordello. You presume to tell me what I must do? The sooner your brother is caught and hanged the better. My own brother is a dunderhead, hopeless at business. I have tried to help him in the past but he has insisted on going his own way. He has brought his misfortunes on himself.'

Hal was feeling more like his old self now that he was bathed and shaved, with clean frock coat. 'I don't think you need to speak to my wife in that manner, señor,' he said.

'You don't, don't you? And who are you, some itinerant gambler? You're not bothered about my nieces. All you're interested in is a cut of whatever ransom is arranged. Show me an American who isn't interested in the almighty dollar. I have yet to meet one.'

'OK,' Hal drawled. 'I'll put my cards on the table. A messenger has arrived to inform me that a ransom of five thousand dollars must be paid in three days. Otherwise the girls will have their throats slit.'

'Charming,' Almedo replied. 'If we still lived in a civilized society I would have you flogged and thrown into prison. You would soon lead us to them. But since we lost the war and our troops were withdrawn, lawlessness disgraces New Mexico. Now honest men must take the law into their own hands.'

'My brother's actions are nothing to do with us,' Teresa cried, stamping her foot. 'Our only aim is to help those girls.'

'And line your own pockets. Well, it's quite out of the question. In spite of appearances, business is not good at the moment. However, I have already spoken to my brother and agreed to help as far as I can. Two thousand in gold. That's all. Where does he want it paid?'

'Two thousand?' Hal stroked back his wavy hair and took a seat, uninvited, at the banqueting table, kicking out his long legs in his polished boots. 'What about me? Surely I am entitled to what you might call a handler's fee. I am the only one who can arrange the handover. I've been given instructions just where to go.'

'You, sir, can do as you wish,' the trader replied, helping himself to a glass of sherry from a decanter but not offering one to Hal, or even suggesting that Teresa be seated. 'If you want a five-hundred dollar fee then Espinosa can have the other fifteen hundred. That is my final word and I consider it a generous one. Good day to you. I will be ready to set off tomorrow at dawn.'

'I dunno,' Hal muttered. 'This is a dangerous mission. How can Espinosa trust you to hand over the cash once he has passed over the girls? It would be better if I took the money to him myself.'

'Ha!' The trader raised the sherry and took a sip. 'Do you really think I am going to hand over two thousand to some ne'er-do-well card cheat? What if you took it into your head to disappear?'

'Those are fighting words, *señor*.' Hal jumped to his feet to restrain Teresa who was letting Almedo have a volley of abuse in salty-sounding Spanish. 'Come on, he ain't gonna change his mind. Let's git outa here.'

'No, I'm certainly not.' Almedo watched Hal drag Teresa away. 'See you tomorrow, Mr Williams. We will go find Espinosa. Don't be late. We want to make an early start.'

★ ★ ★

When they had gone Alfredo settled down with quill and inkpot to write some business letters, including one to the War Office in Washington thanking them for the payment of $3,535.75 received for the successful transportation of arms and equipment to Fort Union — he was paid on the poundage carried — and assuring them he was available with his securely-guarded

130

wagons for any future business.

He also sketched out a poster announcing elections to be held for a town council in Taos, with Ezekiel Simms proposed as mayor. It was important that his future father-in-law should have a main say in affairs, while Alfredo would be behind him representing the Latino population. *All male property-holders of Taos are eligible to vote*, he scrawled. As for the marriage, he would have to put pressure on the miserly shopkeeper to expedite it, with a financial settlement if needs be, before Seth Tobin returned.

Almedo stood and admired himself in the mirror, tall and wiry, a fine head of hair, a brave horseman, a man of substance and standing in the community and of noble birth. Sure, he was hitting 58, but he was still as virile as any man. There was no reason why the girl, if she had any sense, should not agree to a wedding.

The Spaniard buckled on a belt on to which two Rigsby turnaround pistols were hitched, four bullets in each. He practised his draw. No, he had not lost his speed. Almedo was not a violent man, but if Ruth Simms persisted with any romantic hankerings for the backwoods drifter, Tobin, maybe he would have to be enticed into a fight. Almedo and his *vaqueros* would make mincemeat of him.

He went into the chapel to check the contents of his big iron safe which was concealed behind an ornately carved rood screen. The door of the screen was very slightly ajar. Possibly a maid had neglected to close it after dusting. Or could Hal Williams, as he waited his arrival, have been poking around? Maybe the gambler was another one who was looking for an early demise?

The rich trader ate a leisurely luncheon, took a short siesta, but his mind revolved with his plan for the morrow's activity, so about 4 p.m. he strolled over to Aristide's casino. It was already buzzing with Mexicans and Americans drinking at the bar or involved in various games of chance, monte, keno or poker. He noticed two of his own *sabaneros*, attired in colourful Mexican fashion in bright shirts and flared pantaloons. He beckoned one over and told him to ride out to the ranch to tell his son, Gustavo, to come in at first light with half-a-dozen armed men.

Even more gaudy was a bevy of Latino wenches, ostensibly acting as waitresses, very animated as they swished back and forth in their ruched dresses and silk underskirts, holding trays of drinks and refreshments. With their mischievous eyes beneath dark hair they would pause to watch the gaming, leaning over to ensure their low-cut blouses gave an ample display of flesh. Occasionally one would disappear with a client into one of the curtained-off cubicles at the rear. Almedo smiled at a couple he knew, but declined their invitation this afternoon.

Hal Williams was over in a corner, pursing his lips, involved in a game of poker with three Mexican *rancheros* who had come in to town to sell their horses. He figured it was about time to hit them with the two jacks and ace kicker he had slipped his own way when he dealt the cards, Almedo sent a girl over to invite him to join him at the bar.

Hal glanced over, made his strike and lazily grinned at his victims as he rose and raked in the pool of silver pesos and dollars. 'I guess this is mine. Maybe you can try me some other time?'

'I've thought it over and decided to be generous,' Almedo told him. 'There will be two thousand in gold to give Espinosa and this is a banker's draft for five hundred payable to you in seven days' time, only, however, if the transaction is successful.'

'This ain't right,' Hal said. 'I want cash down.'

'Take it or leave it.' Almedo's expression was as hard as carved mahogany. 'Another thing. You know the way to Espinosa's hideout?'

'Roughly,' Hal replied. 'I've been

there, taken under duress, of course. I kept a sharp lookout for any landmarks.'

'Good. I want you to draw me a map as part of the deal.'

'You're joking? Betray my brother-in-law? I'd be signing my own death warrant.'

'He wouldn't be around any more, and I would make sure that you would get the five hundred dollar reward on his head. I wouldn't expect you to go with us up there knowing what a yellow rat you are. Yes or no?'

'Aw, hail,' Hal drawled, 'why not?'

'Good, we will sit down in the corner and I will get you paper and pen.'

'You drive a hard bargain, mister.' Hal pocketed the post-dated cheque. 'You're lucky I ain't a shootin' man.'

When he had scrawled out a map to the best of his memory he passed it to Almedo and watched him make his way over to a table occupied by Kit Carson and Captain Ravilious.

Hal sauntered over to join Teresa at

the bar. 'That wily *haciendado* thinks he can pay me off with peanuts. But I've got plans for him!'

Almedo was busy showing the map to Carson and the captain. 'Can you march your men thirty miles tonight, rest them a few hours and march another thirty tomorrow?'

'I could do, I suppose, if I saw fit.'

'You're an ambitious man, Captain, I know that. If you could kill the most dangerous bandit in the territory I've an idea you would be in line for promotion. I have already mentioned your alacrity and bravery in a letter today to your War Office. Further tributes would follow if we succeed.'

'What plan of action are you proposing?' Ravilious asked.

'First we get my nieces released. Then we make a night attack. We must fool the *renegados* into thinking we have returned to Taos. All I ask is that my gold, which as you know is in this year's newly minted coins paid to me by the War Office, is returned to me if and when recovered. Is that clear?'

He traced a route on the rough map with his index finger and explained his plan further. 'First your troops must cross the desert under cover of darkness; then there is a difficult ascent up through Hell Canyon which Espinosa has closely guarded night and day. What do you think, Captain?'

Ravilious tweaked his moustachios, thoughtfully, and nodded. 'I'm willing to give it a chance.'

'Right, you had better get your men ready to march straightaway. How about you, Kit? You know the mountains well. Are you in?'

'Ah, I wondered why you were letting me in on this military secret.' Carson's square jaw cracked into a grin. 'What's in it for me?'

'I'll pay you a hundred dollars for your time.'

'In that case, why not? Let's drink to victory, gents.'

# 9

They came out of the desert, three men on horse-back, darkly silhouetted like a mirage in the wavering heat-haze. Kit Carson, Alfredo Almedo, and Hal Williams, riding abreast towards the San Isobel forest, its dense evergreens another barrier between them and the sheer parapets of the Sangre de Cristo mountains.

'They got our message,' Carson gritted out through dry lips, for their flashing mirrors had been answered by those on the mountainside. 'They should be here soon.'

Almedo nodded and reached for his wooden canteen, glad to see the end of their blazing hot ten-mile ordeal. He took a sup of the lukewarm water and spat it out. Maybe he was getting too old for this. 'It's up to you now, Hal.'

Williams was relieved to reach firm

terrain after crossing the desert. The return trip had yet to be made, but all he wanted was to get this over with and get out. He took off his hat and wiped sweat from his eyes. 'Where'n hail are they?'

Suddenly *El Borracho* and a line of *bandidos* came as silent as ghosts out of the forest. 'So,' he roared, 'have you come to give us gold? Or to be executed?'

Hal swallowed his fear and nudged his horse forward to parley. 'We have two thousand dollars in gold. That is all they will go to.'

'Two thousand? That is not what we agreed. Still, two thousand is two thousand.' *El Borracho* grinned his broken teeth. 'Let me see it.'

'They won't pass over the gold until you give us the girls. It is no use arguing.'

'Shut your mouth, *gringo*. We could shoot you down like dogs and take it.'

Kit Carson had rode up to join them. 'You could try, fatso, but you'd be the first to go. And we'd take a good many of you down alongside you.'

He swung his mustang around and stretched out a hand at the sand dunes like a master of ceremonies introducing a new act. Out of the haze a band of a dozen *vaqueros* appeared, walking their horses forward, led by Gustavo, who halted beside his father, Almedo.

'So, you'd better go tell Espinosa two thou' is all he's gittin',' Carson said, with a slight smile. 'And to git them gals down here, pronto. We're in no mood fer gabbing.'

*El Borracho* cursed him in Spanish, but hauled his mount around and spurred back into the forest. Long seconds ticked by but eventually Espinosa sauntered his mustang out of the pines, and faced them. Behind him were the two Latino girls scratched and noosed to his rope like captured animals.

'Here they are.' He flashed his mocking smile. 'In pristine condition. I have not touched them. Isn't that so, *muchachas*? Come on, speak up. Your uncle is here with your ransom. But first I must see he does not try to cheat me. Bring him forward.'

When they beckoned to him Almedo trotted his mount forward. 'Keep your trigger fingers at the ready, men,' he called back.

He glowered at Espinosa and took a pouch of many twenty-dollar gold coins from the satchel he carried. He opened the drawstring and tipped them on the ground. 'Count!'

One of the bandits ran forward and, kneeling, greedily picked up the coins, returning them to the pouch. He looked up. 'Eight hundred dollars, *jefe*.'

Almedo produced two more clinking pouches and tossed them to thud on to the ground. 'There's the rest. You must think I'm made of cash. Are you girls all right?'

'*Sí*.' One of them ran forward and grabbed, sobbing, at his boot. 'Thank you, Uncle.'

'Think yourselves lucky we do not kill you all.' Espinosa spat, contemptuously, and stared at Kit. 'You! You are the man Carson I have heard of. If I ever see you in the Sangre de Cristo I will kill you. Beware!'

'You're full of piss and vinegar, pal,' Carson replied. 'You'd better start learnin' how to play the harp. You may be needin' it.'

Espinosa gave a caustic laugh. 'Pleased to do business with you, *hombres*. Next time the price will be higher.'

'Come on,' Almedo said, and began backing his horse away. 'Let's get these girls back to Taos.'

The bandits silently watched until they had reached the *vaqueros* and they all trooped away back into the sand dunes heading towards the setting sun.

Espinosa tossed one of the pouches of gold in his hand and roared with laughter. 'The lousy *gringos*. What cowards they are. Come on, *muchachos*. It is pay day.'

He swirled his mount and galloped

away into the forest as they streamed after him.

* * *

Once out of sight in the great dunes, Carson called a halt. 'Hal, you take the girls home. Tell the captain we'll be waiting for him.'

As Williams and the two girls headed away, the *vaqueros* let their horses nuzzle water poured from canteens into the palms of their hands, and raised blankets on rifles as some sort of shade to shelter under. Carson wriggled forwards like a snake to the crest of a dune and spent a good while peering at the dark, silent forest. When he returned, he snapped out, 'I think it's worked. There's no sign of 'em.'

However, he and his companions sweated it out a while longer as the great ball of sun began to bleed away on to the peaks of the San Juans to the west and slowly disappeared. In its afterglow they carefully moved forward out of the desert and relaxed in the dark shade of the pines.

'How long do you reckon it'll take 'em?' Almedo asked.

Carson chewed on a chunk of beef jerky and drawled, 'Aw, they should be here 'fore midnight. That's if they don't lose their way. You know the army.'

* * *

Captain Ravilious, mounted on his charger, had marched his company of foot soldiers overnight from Taos, given them a four-hour break to eat and catch a bit of sleep, then on again until he reached the strangely shaped pinnacle of rocks Williams had indicated on his map. As the sun began to set he was greatly relieved to see Hal and the two girls come from the desert.

Their father had arrived with horses and there was much hugging and tearfulness as the family was reunited. 'Everything's gone fine,' Hal said, as he and the girls were given food and drink.

'I've done my share. I'm heading back to Taos.'

George Ravilious was too eager for battle to wait for the moon to rise, but had Captain Reynolds assemble his company in marching order, looked at his compass and raised his sabre. 'Forward!'

It would be a hard slog across the dunes, but his nostrils almost twitched at the smell of success. He could hardly wait to see his name in the journals as the man who captured or killed Espinosa.

★   ★   ★

Espinosa laughed as he tossed gold coins to his men and watched them fighting and snarling like dogs, rolling in the dust, snatching up the twenty-dollar cartwheels, only to have them twisted from their fingers.

*El Borracho* laid about him with his brawny arms, pulling men out of the scrum by their hair, throttling one, rabbit-punching another, tossing them aside until he had pocketed a hundred dollars.

When the Mexicans began eye-gouging and pulling knives, screaming threats of death, Espinosa cracked his whip across their backs and brought the scrimmage to a halt. 'Comrades, that is not the way to behave,' he yelled. 'Where is your brotherly love? Save your anger for the *gringos*. Who didn't get any?'

Two of his more puny men crawled from the scrummage, raising their hands like plaintive beggars. 'Well, that will teach you to fight harder next time. You get nothing unless you fight.'

Espinosa went to sit by their big fire, draping a blanket around his shoulders for it got cold at that altitude at nights. He had given them the best part of a thousand dollars. The other thousand he had tucked away into his saddle-bags. The kidnap had paid well, but as he ordered two men to go relieve the guards on the pass, he pondered what his spy, Pedro, had told him when he returned. There was, indeed, a beautiful blonde girl serving in the Simms emporium. It was time he visited Taos himself to take a look at her. The forthcoming fiesta would be good cover as crowds of *peons* flocked into the town from the outlying villages. 'Yes, I will have her for myself,' he vowed. 'Maybe take her back to Mexico. Even when I have had my fill of her some *haciendado* would pay a fortune for such a one.'

★  ★  ★

As the moon rose Gustavo sent his *vaqueros* to scout along the edge of the forest a mile or so in each direction. Eventually the exhausted column of infantry, led by Captain Ravilious and Reynolds, emerged from the dunes, not badly off course.

The punishing forced march of two thirty-mile stints had taken its toll on the recruits, especially the final flounder up and down the dunes, carrying rifle, bayonet, canteen, pack and ammunition, which made their legs feel like lead. All most wanted to do once they had reached the forest, after a meal of hard tack and jerky, was to lie down and sleep. They were allowed only water, not coffee, for no fires were to be built. Nor were they permitted to light pipes or cigarettes.

Indeed, in a low voice Ravilious stressed upon them the need for total silence when they advanced through the forest and up the mountain. Meanwhile, he allowed them to rest until nearly midnight. He planned to hit the bandits when they were least expecting it. Nor had he brought along their twelve-pounder for mules were notorious for their raucous braying which would travel for miles.

'Right, Sergeant,' he snapped, consulting his watch. 'Prepare to move out.'

'Easier said than done,' Murphy muttered, as he kicked and belaboured the snoring men to rouse them. 'Come

148

on, boyos, get on your feet!'

He jabbed his revolver into the temple of one who refused to get up. 'If you don't you'll be put in irons and shot for disobeying an order when we get back. Which is it to be, my lad?'

Not for nothing were they known as 'the poor bloody infantry'. Eventually, resentfully, they were ready, drawn up with muskets at the ready. Now it was the *vaqueros* who protested about leaving their horses and having to proceed on shanks's pony in their high-heeled boots.

The thick bed of pine needles carpeting the forest floor muffled any sound of their march, apart from the cracking of broken twigs. Occasionally Captain Ravilious would call a halt and listen but all to be heard was the mournful hooting of owls or the distant howling of a pack of wolves. On and upwards they went until they emerged from the San Isobel forest and paused below the precipitous cliffs bathed in silver by the moon's glow.

The captain pulled his cape over his head, struck a match and squinted at the map scrawled by Williams. Yes, they seemed to be on the right track. There was a pinnacle of rock that marked the entry to Hell Canyon. 'Total silence from now on,' he hissed back at the men. 'Fix bayonets as quietly as you can. Fire only on the command of the Sergeant-Major. When I give the order to charge, follow me on to glory, boys.'

Almedo nudged his son, Gustavo, and grinned. 'Who the hell does that popinjay think he is?'

But, his ostrich feather in his campaign hat fluttering in the stiff mountain breeze, George Ravilious stealthily climbed up through the rugged terrain, leading them on, revolver at the ready and with his other hand trying to prevent his sabre from clattering against the rocks.

'That idjit's making more noise than the rest of us put together,' Kit Carson growled. 'Maybe we shoulda left the army back home.'

However, they had successfully reached a narrow defile, the one aptly termed Hell Pass, and looking up Ravilious suddenly saw the outline of a sentry, a big sombrero, a rifle in his hand, standing on the peak of a rock which gleamed white as a sugar loaf.

'Shush,' he hissed, raising his hand to stop his column. 'Sergeant, what do you think?'

'I'll go get him, sir.' Murphy returned his revolver to his hoster and buttoned the flap. He produced his eighteen-inch bayonet and wiped a thumb across his throat, giving a wink.

'Wait!' Kit Carson had seen the gleam of a cigarette up on the other bluff. He, too, holstered his revolver and drew a razor-sharp scalping knife. 'That one's mine. When I whistle come as fast as you can.'

'We'll get the buggers, don't you worry, sir. If your honour will kindly bring up our rifles with you when you come,' Murphy stage-whispered. 'And, boys, remember what I taught you on the parade ground.'

'Yes, yes, man,' Ravilious hissed. 'Get on with it.'

He watched the burly sergeant-major's big buttocks straining against his pants as he climbed the steep rocks round the back of the sugar loaf. Carson had loped off in another direction on the other side of the pass.

'They're taking their time,' he muttered. 'What are they playing at?'

'Patience, my friend,' Almedo replied. 'Kit's an expert at this.'

Suddenly there was a sharp squeal of pain from up above on Murphy's side, more like a hunted animal's, followed by a muffled curse. Shortly afterwards a birdlike whistle from Carson's peak beckoned them on.

'Right, follow me, boys,' Ravilious hissed and raised his cocked revolver.

It was about three in the morning. When they negotiated the pass and came out on to the crest of the cliff they saw the ruined Ute fort. Outside, two *renegados*, in ponchos and sombreros were crouched around the embers of a fire, rifles in their hands. The soldiers and *vaqueros* spread out in line, crept forward until they were fifty yards off. Ravilious beckoned them to kneel and take cover to prepare to fire.

Kit Carson wiped clean his bloody knife and returned it to his sheath. He was returned his long-barrelled rifle and, without waiting for the command to fire, put it to his shoulder and squeezed out a ball. The echo of the explosion barrelled away through the ravines. And the head of one of the Mexicans was splattered like a canteloupe melon.

The other guard jumped to his feet, but Gustavo's rifle shot knocked him spinning to lie in a lifeless heap.

Suddenly it was like an antheap had been disturbed. *Bandidos* came running from the fort and pouring out of the holes in the cliffs, hardly big enough to be termed caves.

'Get them!' Ravilious shouted. 'Fire at will, boys.'

As the fusillade from the army and *vaqueros* racketed out, the Mexicans threw up their hands like an agonizied frieze before being toppled. But others had found cover and were returning fire at the flashes of the attackers' guns in the darkness. Wildly, it must be said, and with little effect.

'Reload!' the sergeant-major shouted. 'Give 'em another taste of our lead, lads.'

That was no easy matter. The Springfield rifles, with their forty-inch barrels and weighing ten pounds, had to be muzzle-loaded, the soldiers biting off a paper cartridge and shoving powder and shot down the barrel with the ramrod. 'Take aim, boyos.' The recruits hurried to raise them, fully-cocked to their shoulders. 'Fire!'

The recruits might not have been the best of shots but at that range the hail of .58 calibre bullets did devastating damage. Peering through the black powder smoke they saw more Mexicans go sprawling on their backs.

154

Alfredo Almedo had the chance to use his Rigsby cap 'n' ball turnarounds, loosing the first two barrels of both pistols, and thumbing the mechanism to bring the second set of barrels into the firing position.

'Got him!' he cried, as another *bandido* hit the dust.

Roused from a drunken slumber the Mexicans were confused and panicked. Most had imbibed too much tequila from the barrel to celebrate the handover of the kidnap cash, and Espinosa had joined in the carouse.

'What 'n hell's happening?' he muttered, as he pulled on his boots and buckled his gunbelt.

'We're under attack!' *El Borracho* boomed from the doorway of the tumbledown fort. 'And we're getting the worst of it, *jefe*!' He held his big Volcanic in his fist and crashed out flame and lead sending a trooper tumbling.

Espinosa edged cautiously out behind him and surveyed the scene. 'We've been betrayed,' he hissed. 'This don't look good. Keep firing, *hombre*. We've got to get out.'

He turned to snatch up his saddle-bags, holding the remains of the gold pieces, and his rifle. He came from the fort and loosed bullets from his revolver at the troopers, backing away along the cliff as he did so, screaming, 'Everybody for himself.'

One of his slugs hit Captain Reynolds in the temple, splashing blood and spinning him off his feet. Espinosa always chose the most important target, in this case an officer and, as he moved, he took a potshot at another one in a plumed hat, making him duck down.

But the Rigsby's powerfully propelled lead smashed into the cliff wall, showering him with shards, too close for comfort, and he dashed for cover, climbing over a bluff of the mountain to where their mustangs were tethered.

The bulky *El Borracho* swivelled his eyes, saw him go, and tried to follow, backing away, firing as he went.

Screams of dying, whining ricochets, were left behind as, under cover of the pall of gunsmoke and the night, he scrambled away followed by two other *bandidos*.

Espinosa was already in the saddle as the big man reached him. 'Come on,' he cried, and spurred the horse, sending his mount charging recklessly away, slipping and sliding down a narrow, almost perpendicular path.

'It's all right for him,' *El Borracho* moaned, as he struggled to get aboard his big horse. 'Hold still, you brute. Hey, *jefe*, wait for me. Ride, *muchachos*!'

Back at the fort the battle was almost won as Ravilious raised his sabre and screamed, 'Charge!'

The recruits raced after him, backed by the *vaqueros* and it became bloody close combat, stabbing bayonets against machetes, a maelstrom of fighting, falling bodies.

The spy, Pedro, had left his mustang hitched outside his cave and he, too, tried to escape, vaulting into the saddle and charging towards Hell Canyon. As a young soldier tried to stop him, Pedro slashed him across his throat. But Ravilious gave a backswing of his sabre, knocking him from the saddle. He stuck the steel into his guts, gave a twist and disembowelled him.

The captain wiped blood from the sabre blade and looked about him. 'All right, boys,' he shouted. 'We've won the day.'

A few disarmed Mexicans were cowering back, but most of the two dozen renegados were lying in postures of death, and those wounded were put out of their misery by humane dispatch, as Ravilious termed it.

He strode back to look at Reynolds, who was not a pretty sight, blood running down his face. 'I can't see,' he was crying, clawing at his eyes. The cut to his temple must have severed some optic nerve. 'I'm blind!'

When he heard Ravilious's voice he moaned, 'Please, George, kill me. I can't stand this.'

'You know I can't do that,' his CO replied. 'It's against regulations. We'll patch you up and get you back.'

When Reynolds continued to bemoan his lot, the captain snapped, 'Pull yourself together, man. The misfortunes of war and all that. You'll be invalided out on a full pension. Might even get a medal.'

'Espinosa's got away,' a soldier informed him.

'Yes, I'm aware of that,' Ravilious replied, icily.

'I'll take one of their mustangs and go after him,' Carson told him. 'But I doubt I'll find him. He knows all the goat trails and backpaths of these mountains.'

'It could be worse,' Ravilious cried, still in a state of elation from the life and death struggle. 'We've wiped out this nest of rats, nineteen of 'em, taken three prisoners — we'll hang 'em in Taos — with only ten casualties of our own, four dead, six wounded. My congratutlations to you all, gentlemen.'

As a reward to the troops he ordered the barrels of tequila they found to be broken open and food to be cooked. All gold coins of that year's date found on the Mexicans were to be returned to Señor Almedo. But all other property, cash, guns, horses, would be split among the lower ranks as fortunes of war.

The sergeant-major's ruddy face split into a grin. 'Sounds like we're gonna have quite a party, my brave boys. But ye've earned it. Ye're true soldiers now.'

'That's all very well,' Almedo told Gustavo after $650 in gold coin was returned to him. 'But this isn't much. There's a thousand four hundred missing. Come on, let's leave them to it and get back.'

Murphy watched them go and winked at his squaddies, revealing a gold cartwheel glinting between his fingers. 'Here's one that rich greaser didn't get.'

# 10

Taos was deathly quiet when Hal Williams rode in. The army and *vaqueros* were away in the mountains. It was siesta time. He hitched his horse outside the town hotel, climbed the stairs to their room and entered quietly. Teresa was lying naked under a sheet on the bed, her Mayan face serene, her black hair spread out across the pillow. '*Mi amor*,' she murmured, raising bronzed arms to him. 'You are back. You look exhausted. Come to bed.'

'Ain't got time for that.' Hal was in an agitated state. He took a slug from a bottle of bourbon, splashed water on his face and found a clean shirt. 'This is my big chance. I'm gitting out. You wanna come you better git dressed. Here' — he tossed her a gold coin — 'go buy two fresh horses, some basic supplies for the journey; have 'em ready to ride.'

Teresa sat up, hugging her bare breasts. 'Where are you going?'

'I got business. It won't take long.' He took a revolver from a drawer, checked the cylinder to ascertain it was loaded. 'Fill the canteens and wait for me by the fountain.'

His next call was to a store that sold mining equipment where he purchased a keg of gunpowder and fuse wire. With it under his arm he strode along to Señor Almedo's house and hammered on the big oak door. When it was opened by a maid he pushed inside and stuck the revolver under her nose. 'Don't make a sound. Come with me.'

In the chapel he opened the ornate wooden rood screen, shoved the barrel of gunpowder under the legs of the big iron safe, threaded the fuse wire back out to the safety of the banqueting room, knelt and found his vesta case in his frock-coat pocket. He struck a match and winked at the frightened girl.

The whole house reverberated as the gunpowder barrel went up. Maids, servants, grooms came running from the kitchen and other rooms. Hal waggled the six-gun at them and indicated they should step into the chapel. 'One false move from any of you and she gets it,' he drawled, putting the gun to the girl's head.

As the powdersmoke swirled they gasped to see the debris in the chapel. The safe had toppled to one side, its door hanging open. 'Fantastic,' Hal cried, reaching in to stuff the carpet bag he had brought with greenbacks, pesos, and gold coins. When it was full he stood and grinned at them. 'A friggin' fortune. So long, folks. Give my regards to Almedo.'

He backed out, took the big key from the front door as he left, locked it from the outside, and hurried away as people called out asking what had happened.

'C'mon,' he cried to Teresa, now clad in a stiff-brimmed hat and riding outfit. He climbed on to the horse she had brought. 'We'll head past the Eagle's Nest, over Raton Pass and down the Purgatoire River.'

As Aristide came from his casino he saw the gambler and his girl go galloping away out of town. 'They sure seem to be in a hurry,' he mused. 'What they been up to?'

★   ★   ★

Seth Tobin was not having a lot of luck. It was a winding, rocky and tough trail he had to negotiate from Cañon City. He was heading into Ponca Springs when he heard an ominous crack and a wheel went flying as the wagon swung to one side, keeling over and bringing the horses to a halt.

'The damn axle's broken,' he muttered, as he jumped down and took a look. 'I'm gonna have to go back to town and git Clarence to come out and give me a hand. I'll never repair this on my own.'

He unharnessed the wagon horses,

hobbled their front legs so they could hop around and graze, and swung on to Star. 'Only hope the thievin' Utes don't steal all my stuff while I'm gone'

It would be a thirty-mile ride back to Cañon City along the Arkansas. 'C'mon, boy, let's git. This ain't a good start.'

★   ★   ★

After being allowed a day of rest and recreation the army had slogged back to Taos with their three prisoners, bearing their injured on stretchers of pine boughs. Captain Reynolds, whose blindness appeared permanent, was given every comfort and assured by Ravilious that he would return with him to Fort Union to make his report.

First, however, George Ravilious wanted to enjoy himself that weekend as the Mexicans were about to commence their fiesta and the town was buzzing with people. There would be the Sunday processions and services devoted to the memory of the Virgin of Guadaloupe. But on the Monday the town would erupt with singing and dancing.

'I'll give 'em a special treat and hold a public hanging of those three criminals,' the captain told his sergeant-major. 'It will act as a warning to any others who think of following the ways of banditry.'

'Yes, sor,' Murphy beamed, saluting smartly. 'Folks love a good hanging.'

'Poor old Almedo. Seems like he's been robbed in our absence. He claims he's ruined.' Ravilious couldn't restrain a smile for it might well put the old Spaniard out of the running as a suitor for the Simms girl. In fact, he had been thinking that although she had no dowry or social standing, Ruth might well be a suitable wife for him. He was not getting any younger and it was time he made the jump. 'I must confess I'm quite smitten by the hussy,' he said, as he bathed and dressed in his best uniform.

Alfredo was in Aristide's drowning his sorrows. It had been a dreadful shock to find his house in such a mess, most of his cash, thousands of dollars, swept from his safe. From what Aristide said it seemed the miscreants were headed south to Santa Fe so he had sent Gustavo and his *vaqueros* in pursuit.

'Don't you worry, *señor*.' Aristide refilled his wine glass. 'Those two won't get away.'

Alfredo had decided to stay behind, not only because he was wearied by the long ride, but because as the only *hidalgo* in the area he would be expected to attend church services and preside over the dancing and festivities to be held in the casino the following evening.

In his father's day he would have had *droit de seigneur*, would have reigned over his peons like a feudal lord. In return the house servants and *vaqueros* would have been looked after from birth to death.

'Times have changed,' he said. 'When the *vaqueros* got too old to work I would have made them my pensioners. But, no, they want to do it the American way now. They want a monthly wage of ten dollars. What will they do with it? Spend it on drink. Can you see any of them putting anything aside for old age? I doubt it.'

'Still,' Aristide consoled, 'if that's what they want it lets you off the hook.'

'Possibly.' The trader had seen Ravilious in his feathered hat, heading for the Simms store. 'What's he up to? Sniffing around Ruth's skirts? He'll no doubt spread rumours about me.'

For her part Ruth was growing weary of being plagued by her suitors. Ravilious had knelt before her in the parlour to propose marriage, seeming to assume she could not refuse such an honour, wanting to seal it with frantic kisses she tried to avoid. What, be stuck in some dusty frontier fort, bearing the children of such an opinionated man?

'War will surely come,' he assured

her, as if that was to be welcomed. 'The southerners are refusing to give up their slaves. There's trouble ahead. It's bound to be a wonderful opportunity for promotion. I might even make general. Think of that, my dear.'

'I'd rather not,' she replied, making an excuse to wriggle out of his clutches.

Senor Almedo, in spite of his troubles, was just as amorous. He had assured Simms there would still be a couple of thousand in it for him, plus the prestige, if he persuaded her to walk down the aisle with him in a week or two.

'Don't it worry you, her being a Protestant? Well, she ain't in my opinion, just an out-and-out heathen. You're welcome to her,' Ezekiel said, 'Just as soon as I see your cash.'

He cornered Ruth and reminded her that he couldn't afford to keep another female; she wasn't needed in the store, and had better accept Almedo's offer pretty smart. On his instructions Mildred constantly nagged her about it, too.

'But what about Seth?' she cried, the memory of his kiss still fresh in her memory. 'I can't just — '

'Aw, you've seen the last of him,' Simms screeched. 'He's a wild, uneddi-cated, no-good mountain man. Don't kid your sen, niece, he'll never settle down. He'll be away to the hills. Anyhow I've heard he's already wed to some Shoshoni girl. Probably got a teepee full of half-caste brats. That's the sort of man he is.'

This statement certainly gave the girl food for thought. Could it be true? He had spoken about living with the Shoshoni. He may have kissed her, but he had not made any promises. Would he, she began to wonder, ever come back?

★ ★ ★

Hal shivered with cold as he held a tin mug of coffee in his hands. They had spent an uncomfortable night camped on the shore of the Eagle's Nest Lake. He had hardly slept at all, having a horror not only of snakes and creepy-crawlies, but of the prospect of bears and cougars prowling the dark woods around them. And an owl, that bird of evil omen, had hooted mournfully all night. Now the sun was rising, turning the 4,000 foot icy pinnacles above them ablaze with its rays. They had come about thirty-five miles from Taos. His plan was to strike north, hit the Oregon Trail and take passage with a wagon train to the west coast and safety.

'We got a hell of a way to go,' he moaned.

'We can make it.' Teresa was made of sterner stuff, having spent all her life in such harsh climes. 'Come on, let's move. Just think, Hal, when we get to California we'll be rich.'

They cantered their horses onwards but, as they climbed the trail away from the lake and rounded a corner, Hal's life seemed to drain from him. 'No, it can't be,' he whispered, his mouth going dry. From over the ridge four horsemen were coming, darkly silhouetted against the crimson sky of the dawn. Hal squinted into the sun's rays — seeing the flash of silver on spurs and bridle, the wide brimmed sombreros, the fiery mustangs. 'How did they get away?'

Hal's blood turned to ice. He wanted to turn and take flight, but he knew that would be no use. He forced himself to go on and meet them. Maybe he could bluff his way out. 'Howdy,' he called, but he heard his voice quaver.

'*Hola!*' Espinosa reined in, his lips curling back in a snarling smile. 'Who do we have here? My dear sister. And my brother-in-law. What fortune. Just the ones I wished to meet. Can these be the slimy slugs who crawled to the captain of the blue-coats and told them where they could find me?'

'That's not true.'

'Shut up.' *El Borracho* moved his horse up close and smashed the back of his fist into Hal's jaw. 'Hey, what's this?'

He grabbed the bulging carpet bag hung from the pommel of Hal's saddle and held it aloft. 'Looks like the gambling man has been a bad boy.'

'I broke into Almedo's house, blew his safe, stole his gold. I told you I would be working for you,' Hal stuttered. 'We were coming to find you. There's a fortune. We can all share it fair and square.'

The two *compañeros*, the only other two to have escaped the army assault, gathered round and gave shrill cackles of glee as *El Borracho* trickled gold and silver coins through his fingers. One crossed himself, crying, 'Praise be to the Virgin of Guadaloupe. She has looked down on us this day.'

'*Sí*, praise be,' Espinosa said, but there was malevolence in his dark eyes. 'No doubt my dear sister will also claim that she knew nothing of the filthy treachery that left all our comrades dead?'

Teresa remained impassive, sat immobile in her dark riding outfit, holding her whip in her hands. She met her brother's eyes. 'What does it matter? We can all be rich now. You can go back to Mexico. We will go on to California.'

Espinosa swept off his sombrero to hold it across his midriff. 'At least, Teresa, you are not fool enough to deny your treachery, unlike this piece of offal.'

Hal saw that the game was over. While the Mexicans were distracted gloating over the contents of the carpet bag he played his last card. He shook the small derringer out of his sleeve and aimed point blank at Espinosa. But before he could even fire, flame and lead burst through the crown of the sombrero and Hal screamed in agony, clutching his shattered wrist.

Espinosa laughed manically. 'Now you will have to try your cheating tricks with your left hand. Did you really think you could get me with that pea-shooter?'

He fired his revolver again and the slug took out Hal's left elbow. He screamed as lariats were tossed over him and he was dragged from the saddle. The two bandits charged away, dragging him through the dust, thorns and rocks. His hair, face and body were torn and bloodstreaked when he was returned.

'What shall we do?' *El Borracho* roared. 'Let him live a cripple? Or use him as target practice?'

'We have wasted too many bullets already because of him. And ruined my good hat.' Espinosa pulled his knife from his crimson sash, rode up to Hal and deftly slit his throat.

Teresa made no sound as she watched her husband's eyes glaze over and his head slump. She turned defiantly to Espinosa. 'You cannot kill me. I am your blood. God would punish you.'

'Can't I?' The bandit smiled, devilishly. 'No, but the others can. Hey, comrades, you want her? Take her into the woods. Do what you want with her.'

Teresa screamed as she was dragged

from her horse by *El Borracho* and the yelping bandits jumped from their mustangs and grabbed hold of her.

Espinosa caught *El Borracho*'s arm. 'Have fun with her. Rape her. Beat her. But don't kill her. Let her crawl on her knees back to Taos. She is no longer my sister. That *puta* is fit only for the whorehouse.'

# 11

Ezekiel Simms's beady eyes glinted with malicious pleasure as he ordered his daughters to hang on to Ruth while the Mexican barber trimmed her blonde hair urchin short. 'Hold the hussy still,' he shrilled, 'or she'll git her ears nicked orf.'

He picked up the long shorn tresses and remarked, 'We could turn this into a wig and sell it in the shop to some bald ol' frump.'

'If you do I want the cash,' Ruth gritted out. 'It's my hair.'

'A woman's role is silence and obedience,' he lectured her. 'It's about time you larned that. Take her away and scrub her hard, scrub the nonsense out of her.'

He grinned some more as he listened to Ruth's squawks of protest as she was forced into a big tub of steaming water and attacked with brushes and black carbolic soap. 'That'll do her good,' he told the barber, paying him his quarter.

When they were done he had her dressed in coarse calico drawers, a matching bodice and a dowdy dress of homespun, one of Mildred's cast-offs, practically threadbare. 'Now,' he said, spitefully, assessing her, 'you look clean enough to visit God's church.'

Crammed amid identically attired women and girls in the little Baptist church the loathsome sunbonnet she was forced to wear was the last straw. She clamped her teeth resolutely tight as all around yelled, '*What a friend we have in Jesus.*'

'You're welcome to Him,' she whispered. 'I'd prefer a few friends in *this* world.'

'It seems as if Cousin Ruth is gradually learning to behave in a fit and proper way,' Simms remarked the next night at supper, unaware of what rebellious thoughts were seething in her head. 'She can be excused doing the dishes tonight.'

Instead, Mildred found her a pile of darning to do as they listened to the other girls clattering the pots in the scullery.

The poky-nosed dowd herself was attending to a new dress of pink candy-stripe draped over a tailor's dummy. 'Aren't these newfangled safety pins a wonder,' Mildred exclaimed. 'Begone pricked fingers!'

'Yes, wonderful,' Ruth replied, half-heartedly. She wondered who the lucky girl was to be bought such a pretty dress, its quite daringly low-cut neck-line trimmed with lace. 'It sounds like the Mexicans are celebrating their *fiesta*.'

There was a lot of noise and merriment coming from the plaza, the clatter of hoofs as folks rode in from outlying village's, the sound of clapping and castanets as they joined in some spontaneous dancing, loud pistol shots or explosions of gunpowder hammered on anvils.

'Señor Almedo invited me to their ball,' Ruth pursued. 'If you want to marry me off to him I don't see why you should object.'

'Heavens, where is your modesty, girl?' Mildred exclaimed. 'It is far too early for that yet.'

'Listen to the racket,' Ezekiel said, coming in with an armful of logs, for on the plateau it got cold at nights. 'That just proves what a bunch of devil-worshippers these people are. They've been parading their idolatrous painted statues around the plaza all day, now they're going to get pig drunk. I'd better lock the shutters tonight.'

'Why shouldn't they celebrate?' Ruth chimed in. 'It gives them a rest from their toil. Tomorrow they'll be back in the fields again.'

'There is nothing so destroys a man as strong liquor. For a woman to partake is an abomination against the Lord. Thank God this family is a sober, righteous one.'

'Amen,' Mildred agreed.

To reinforce his point, Ezekiel quoted Proverbs, 'Wine *is a mocker, strong drink is raging, and whosoever is deceived thereby is not wise.*'

Ruth protested, 'I can't see how a little drinking and dancing, in moderation, does any harm.'

'That's enough!' Ezekiel shrieked. 'Beware, Ruth, of such ungodly thoughts. You are courting shame and folly. Beware the pit of flames, girl. Go to your room and pray for deliverance.'

'Yes, I'll pray for deliverance,' Ruth murmured, as she went to the bedroom she shared with the girl and undressed. 'Deliverance from you, you mangy miserable sod.'

It was torment to the girl to have to lie abed beside the other three females in the darkened stuffy room and listen to the carnival carousal in the streets outside. 'Am I really wicked?' she wondered. 'Well, if they say so, why shouldn't I be?'

The thought of the tall frontiersman, Seth, filled her mind, the touch of his lips, the way he held her close that night. But he was far away, footloose and fancy free, no doubt enjoying himself. He had given no indication that he wanted her to be his bride, just rode off on his horse with a wave of his hand.

'I must get out,' she whispered, raising herself as if gasping for lungfuls of air. 'This place is driving me crazy.'

She was on the edge of the bed nearest to the door and she swung her bare feet to the floor-boards. Suddenly Rebecca woke and clung to her nightgown sleeve. 'What's the matter, Ruth?'

Ruth glanced across her at the two younger girls, but they were fast asleep. Ezekiel's shrill snores were penetrating from the adjoining room where he was ensconced in his double bed with Mildred. 'I'm going to the dance,' she whispered. 'Will you come with me?'

'What?' Rebecca's eyes opened wide in her pudgy face. 'Are you mad?'

'Possibly. Come on. Let's have some

fun. I can't go on my own; I need you with me. Put your best dress on and hurry.'

'What are *you* going to wear?'

Ruth put her index finger to her lips and smiled. 'You'll see.'

The door creaked as she opened it and slid out into the corridor. She froze but Simms kept snoring. She crept to the living-room, carefully removed the pink candy-stripe from the dummy, stripped off her nightgown, and wriggled naked into the crisp, tight-fitting material. She glanced in the mirror. 'Golly gee, can that be me? How saucy!' She twirled around, buttoning the bodice, found her soft slippers. They would have to do for want of better. She ran fingers through her short locks and covered them with a white mantilla.

'Gosh, Ruth, you look really heavenly,' Rebecca cooed, mouth open with amazement. 'I wish I — '

'You look fine,' Ruth assured her. She dowsed the candle and carefully unlocked the front door of the shop, opening it to peer out. 'The coast's clear. Come on.'

'This is crazy.' Rebecca had a terrified look on her face. 'What if — '

'Oh, you and your what ifs. What can he do? He can't make our lives much more miserable. Come on. Hurry. We won't be away long.'

As her tubby cousin squeezed out, Ruth closed the door quietly, and smiled brazenly. 'See! We're free for an hour or two. Isn't it great?'

Rebecca didn't seem so convinced, but she hung on to her arm as they hurried out into the plaza. 'Listen to all that noise. Where is the dance?'

'Over at Aristide's place.'

'We can't go in there.'

'Why not?'

'Oh, dear.' Rebecca giggled as a cluster of Mexican youths serenaded them with guitars as they crossed the plaza. 'Ooh, no, we can't stop. We're going to the dance.'

'Come on, here we are. Let's go in.'

Normally a single girl wouldn't have

dared enter such a house of ill repute. But tonight the gaming tables had been pushed to one end of the casino to provide a platform for a band of grinning Mexicans, who were strumming away madly at guitars, drums and mandolins.

Tonight the Latino population had taken over, a small charge imposed to keep out riff-raff. There were numerous black-haired, coffee-hued maidens in all their finery, accompanied by their mamas or stately *duennas*. Among them the paler and fair-haired Ruth was striking in contrast.

'They're looking at us,' Rebecca squawked. 'They're bound to tell Father tomorrow in the store.'

'Nonsense. They're happy to see us, that's all.' Ruth smiled gaily about her as they found chairs. 'Why worry about *mañana*.'

There was such a crescendo of sound, and spectacle of colour as the musicians made their shrill, whirring screams. The thump of hand-heels on instrument board summoned ideas of wild horsemen galloping in a reckless charge. Out on the floor before them was a frenzy of dancers doing the fandango; *caballeros* in fancy shirts and silver-flashing, flared trousers, stamped their high-heeled boots proudly, as *señoritas* swirled their dazzling silk dresses like graceful fans, giving glimpses of silk-stockings and rolled their dark eyes, amid clacketing castanets and cries from the watching throng of '*Olé! Vaya! Viva!*' The two excited American girls had seen nothing like it. There was music and laughter wherever they turned.

'Goodness!' Ruth shouted through the din, watching men at the bar tossing Taos whiskey and tequila down their throats as if they had money to burn. 'I wouldn't have missed this for worlds.'

A slightly inebriated youth, with tousled black curls and eyes to match, weaved towards her, bowed with gross exaggeration, taking Ruth's hand and pulling her into the next dance. The music exploded and she was whirled away in a *sarabando*, doing her best to follow the steps.

'Hey, look at that!' Aristide cried, spotting her. 'Isn't she the shopkeeper's girl? How would you like to give *her* a gallop?'

Señor Almedo stood by his side in a tight-fitting, short-jacketed, velveteen suit and ruffled shirt. He followed his gaze and his lofty features registered alarm. 'Be careful what you say,' he warned. 'You are speaking of my *proyecto de amor.*'

His love project suddenly met his staring eyes, as she was whirled by, smiled and fluttered her fingers.

'What on earth is she doing here?' Alfredo shouted, 'on her own? Has the storekeeper gone mad?'

'Per'aps he don't know,' Aristide chuckled.

The dance was ending and the youth escorted Ruth back to her cousin. Almedo unbuckled his gunbelt and put the heavy brace of Rigsbys behind the bar. 'I'll teach that young monkey.' He picked up a bottle of wine and two glasses. 'Thinks he can muscle in on my fiancée.'

He pushed through the crush and nudged the Mexican boy with his elbow. 'You dance with the other one.'

'She's too fat for me,' the boy protested, but did as he was told and sat down beside Rebecca.

'Good evening,' Alfredo greeted Ruth. 'This is a surprise.'

Ruth smiled broadly. 'Fancy meeting you here, *señor*. I would have thought you were too old for such sport.'

'Don't be cheeky, young lady. I would have thought you would be too young. Doesn't your uncle retire to bed early? How did you persuade him to let you out unchaperoned?'

Ruth shrugged and accepted a glass of wine. 'You know the maxim, what the eye don't see, the heart don't grieve over. We're being rather naughty, I must admit.'

'Damnably foolish, in my opinion.

There are some nefarious characters around. Dangerous and drunken — '

'And you're willing to protect me from them?' Ruth knocked the wine back in two gulps. It was delicious. She twirled her glass by the stem. 'Don't worry, Alfredo, nobody's going to hurt me.'

Almedo glanced at the tremble of her pale breasts almost bursting from the low-slung neck-line, and groaned inwardly. 'God protect us!' he murmured. 'You know not what you do.'

He refilled her glass and had to shout to be heard above the din. Another fandango had begun. 'It is so noisy here. Why don't we go back to my house?'

'Oh, yes?' Ruth raised her eyebrows, mockingly, and stroked a hand through her short golden hair. 'What exactly would you have in mind there? No, I just want to dance, Alfredo. Come on.' She took him by the arm and pulled him into the whirl. 'Let's see if you're as young as you claim.'

With a clatter of hoofs Espinosa rode into Taos with his three companions. They weaved their way through the clumps of *peons* who couldn't afford admission to Aristides, or perhaps preferred the less formal atmosphere out on the plaza. Whatever, they were holding their own little parties, singing, strumming, clapping, dancing. All day Sunday they had borne their cumbersome shrines around the streets in procession, some even grovelling on their knees, flaying themselves in penance, praying in their church to the Virgin. But today, Monday, full of cheap and fiery liquor they were having an ecstatically good time.

*El Borracho* beamed about him. 'With all this racket going on they ain't going to notice us, *jefe*.'

Espinosa sprang from his mount. 'You wait outside. You other two go buy five fresh horses along at the corral.' He tossed one a gold piece. 'Have them saddled and ready. We may need to get out of here fast.'

He passed the bulging carpet bag to the big man. 'Strap this to one of the fresh horses and be ready to ride.'

The tall bandit chief had enquired about the whereabouts of the blonde *Americano* girl from a bunch of youths who said they had seen her go into the casino.

He pushed inside and paid an old man at the door a quarter. 'You must hand your revolver in at the bar, *señor*,' he whined.

Espinosa nodded, tipped his bullet-torn sombrero on to his back, and casually made his way across the floor. The place was dimly lit by guttering candles, and one or two hurricane lamps. There was a haze of *cigarillo* smoke and everybody was so animated none noticed him. He had had a long dusty ride that day and he needed a beer. '*Cervesa*,' he called, and turned to survey the scene.

The new bar-keep assumed the

*caballero* must have surrendered his gun and slid a glass of beer his way, in a hurry to deal with others of the thirsty throng.

Ruth Simms was recuperating from her exertions with the elderly Mexican on the dance floor.

Rebecca was wriggling and protesting in the arms of the amorous curly-haired youth. 'Where's Señor Almedo?' she asked.

'He said he had to go to shake hands with a neglected friend,' Ruth replied, mischievously adding, 'whatever that means. He told me not to run away. Who does he think I am, Cinderella?'

'Perhaps we ought to get back?'

'No.' The youth squeezed the girl to him, giving her a flurry of kisses. 'You heard her. She must wait for her old man.'

'Hm.' Ruth made a downturned grimace. She didn't like the sound of that. But at least Alfredo was *safe*.

Suddenly the music was starting up again and a strong, bronzed hand gripped her arm, pulling her to her feet — a tall, handsome Mexican, with gleaming white teeth. 'You dance with me, *señorita*.'

It wasn't so much a question as an order as, spurs jangling, he whirled her out onto the floor and joined the promenade. 'It is true,' he cried. 'I could not believe my eyes.'

'What do you mean?' she faltered as he spun her around and held her close to him. Too close for comfort, in fact. His mass of dark hair hung across his mahogany brow, and his dark eyes burned into hers. There was mockery in their coal-black depths and lechery in his smile. 'Please, don't hold me so tight. I can hardly breathe.'

'Yes, you take my breath away, too. I could not believe what they told me, that an angel had descended from heaven,' he said in his husky, broken English. 'But now I see it is true.'

Ruth wasn't so sure she liked this. There was something about him that made her insides quake. There was a menace in his eyes. And he danced with her in too familiar a fashion, one hand grabbing her buttock, naked beneath the thin candy-stripe dress, one knee thrusting between her legs as he swept her around the floor. Suddenly a hot flush of panic gripped her. Somehow he reminded her of that other Mexican, the big, bearded one, who had torn her dress apart. She could sense people watching them and her face coloured up as she struggled to be free.

'That's enough,' she cried. 'I have to take my friend home.'

'I have come for you, Ruth. You are ver' beautiful,' he growled, his massive shoulders hugging her into him, holding her close to his chest, his mouth whispering in her ear. 'You know you want me, my angel. This is destiny. It is no use fighting. You must be mine.'

'How do you know my name?' She tried to hold back as he waltzed her towards the door. 'Who are you?'

'Who you theenk I am?'

'Espinosa!' Señor Almedo had returned

to the casino after relieving himself outside. Shocked to see the girl in the bandit's arms he had struggled to pull one of his Rigsbys from beneath the bar, and flourished it wildly. 'Let her go. I order you.'

For reply the tall bandit swung Ruth before him as a shield. 'What you going to do about it?' he shouted, and fired his revolver from beneath her arm.

There were screams and shouts as the shot crashed out and Almedo went spinning back crashing into the bottles at the back of the bar. He hit the floor, clutching a bloody wound in his chest amid a shower of glass.

*El Borracho* suddenly came smashing on his mustang through the flimsy casino doors, charging into the dance hall, almost knocking Espinosa flying. He fired his revolver like a maniac in all directions and the unarmed men and girls dived for cover.

'You fool, what are you playing at?' Espinosa managed to dodge behind the kicking hoofs, hugging Ruth into him. He cursed *El Borracho* for an idiot, but at least the intrusion covered his escape.

Outside he slung her unceremoniously over the neck of his horse and leaped into the saddle behind her. He whirled around, shooting over the heads of the crowd to quell any interference. 'Bring the spare horses,' he shouted to the two *compañeros*.

*El Borracho* came crashing back out of the casino, guffawing and grinning. 'Look,' he shouted, pointing to a parade of *peons* who had come to a halt holding tar flares over their heads. 'Let's have some fun, *jefe*.'

He galloped away and snatched two flaming brands from the *peons*' hands. 'Why not?' Espinosa grinned and followed his example, snatching a flare as he cantered past, hanging on with the other hand to the captive, screaming girl. He hurled it smashing through the window of the Simms emporium and rode laughing on his way. 'Burn them down,' he yelled.

*El Borracho* and the other two

*bandidos* followed his example, sending the torches spinning to land inside the tinder-dry timber houses and stores of the *gringos*. The one thrown by Espinosa had landed in a barrel of molasses and there were screams as the Simms shop burst into flames.

'I warned them,' Espinosa screamed.

Captain Ravilious came running from the hotel, leaping down the steps and aimed his revolver at the Mexicans. The bullet hit one and, with a burning pain in his side, he fell forward, hanging onto his mustang's neck.

Espinosa rode back to cover them, and fired three shots at the army captain, making him roll for cover beneath the sidewalk. As the slugs whanged past him the captain peered out and saw the blonde girl's tormented face as she kicked and wriggled trying to escape. Fearing he might hit her he dared not fire in reply.

The bandit leader gave him a leering grin and wave, turned and galloped after his men. Ravilious scrambled out and aimed a last shot at his back, but he was by now too far off. He watched them reach the end of the street and disappear into the night.

'Oh, my God,' he groaned. 'They've got her this time.'

# 12

Señor Alfredo Almedo lay in his bed, listening to the gurgle of his lungs, hovering on the doorstep 'twixt life and death as the army surgeon prepared to cut out the bullet from his chest. 'I'll increase the reward on Espinosa to two thousand dollars,' he rasped out. 'Dead or alive.'

Gustavo had returned from a wild goose chase and vowed to go after him as soon as a posse was raised. The *vaqueros* had no beef with the *bandido*. Indeed some in the past had been tempted to join him. But such a reward was a fortune.

Those troopers who could ride were assembled by Captain Ravilious, mounted on commandeered steeds, and joined by several irate settlers. Ezekiel Simms stared at the ashes of his store and hissed at his wife, 'It's all that Ruth's fault. I hope she burns in Hell.'

Kit Carson came loping on his horse into town with the torn and bleeding Teresa hanging to him. 'If he does this to his sister God knows what he'll do to that poor girl,' he said. 'Come on, boys, let's get after them.'

★　★　★

Espinosa rode across the silver sage up to a dusty spur of yucca and stunted junipers. He turned in the saddle to look back at the cloud of dust being kicked up by the posse. 'Damn them,' he cried. 'Won't they ever give up?' For three days now they had hung on his tail. Whenever he thought they had gone back there they were again.

He had been tempted to cut back across the big desert and take refuge in his old hideout, but he knew they would follow him. So he had kept his men pounding north towards the Arkansas River.

Ruth, her wrists chafed by rawhide

bonds tied in front of her so she could hang on to the reins, aching and dusty, her thin dress rucked up revealing her bare legs, stared into her unpromising future and suggested, 'Maybe if you discarded me they would give up.'

'No chance, sweetheart. I am rich man.' He laughed harshly. 'I take you back to old Mexico. You will live like a princess with me.'

He licked his dry lips with a flicker of lust as he looked at her. She had fought like a mad cat the first night they called a halt and he tried to have her. But he had been disconcerted by thoughts of pursuit, weary of constant riding. Soon, though, he would break her in like a wild horse, gentle her so she would beg for his touch.

He kissed his bunched fingertips and leered at her. 'Don' worry, *mi amor*. Soon you will be bathed and perfumed and I will make love to you on a bed of silken sheets. I promise you, you will be mine.'

'That ain't fair, *jefe*. I saw her first,'

*El Borracho* butted in. 'You said we could have a go at the bitch, too.'

'Shut up, you slop pan. When we get back to Mexico I may even make her my wife.'

The *compañero* who had been shot in the side groaned and slowly slid from his horse. He lay on the ground, his eyes pleading, clutching his blood-stained shirt. 'Don't leave me, *jefe*. They will hang me.'

'They will not do that to one of my men.' Espinosa pulled out his revolver, thumbed the hammer, leaned over and splattered the man's brains. He shrugged. 'I had to. He would slow us up. Come on. Forward! Not far now to the river. We will escape down the ravine and follow the outlaw trail home.'

He jerked at the noose around Ruth's neck. 'Ride, woman. *Arriba! Arriba!*'

★　★　★

Seth Tobin had been forced to kick his heels for a few frustrating days in

Cañon City. Clarence Williams had taken a look at the shattered wagon and decided it was beyond repair. So they had loped all the way back again.

'Don' you worry, massuh,' the black man said. 'I found an ol' flatbed in the blacksmith's yard. I'll do that up fo' you. Only it'll take a little time.'

Seth was cleaning his five-shot revolver, washing it in a pail of water before oiling, and made desultory small talk with Jack Jackson, who was hanging over the bar, unsteadily, already three sheets to the wind.

'The reason I like this gun,' he said, 'is 'cause it don't have a trigger guard. In the snows I don't need to take my glove off to shoot it.'

He had restocked his leather belt-pouch with two tins of ammunition, one of forty combustible .38s for the Paterson, another forty .52s for the Sharps.

Rancid Rita chewed languidly on gum and drawled, 'You men, allus lookin' fer a fight. Why cain't you relax?'

Seth was fretting at the bit to get

away from that place and their company. 'I wish I could,' he said.

There was the sound of horses arriving outside, not unusual at this time of day, the late afternoon. The young frontiersman looked up from his task to see who the new arrivals were. His jaw dropped, speechless, as he stared at them.

'*Hola, amigos!*' Espinosa kicked open the batwing doors of the saloon and dragged the dishevelled Ruth in with him by the rawhide noose around her neck. He brandished the revolver in his right fist, checking the few occupants, who didn't appear to pose any threat. 'Tequila, barman, for me and my ladyfriend.'

A Mexican, clad in greasy leathers and toting a rifle in their direction, came in behind them. 'It is all quiet down the street,' he said in Spanish.

'*Bueno.*' Espinosa tipped tequila into three tumblers from a bottle and pushed one before her. 'Drink. Go on. Do as I say.'

'I'd rather have a drink of water,' the girl croaked out, her eyes meeting Seth's. She raised her bound wrists to remove the dead bandit's sombrero which Espinosa had told her to wear to 'protect her beautiful white skin'.

'Drink,' Espinosa snarled, so she took a sip of the fiery liquor. The *jefe* grinned and tousled her fair shorn hair. 'It will put you in a loving mood.'

Talk about being caught with my pants down, Seth thought. His revolver was out of commission in the pail of water and his Sharps in the blanket roll behind his saddle. And he had left Star along at the livery. His only weapon was the knife on his belt. He got to his feet slowly from the box he had been sitting on and eased his fingers back to feel for it. One throw at Espinosa when he took a drink and a quick dive at the one with the rifle. He tensed himself in readiness.

'What you got that rope round that poor gal's neck fer?' Jack Jackson slurred. 'Wha' ya doin' that fer, you lousy greaser?' He made a move to get off his stool as if to throw a punch.

Espinosa hardly blinked. His revolver barked out as fast as a bolt of lightning and, as the black acrid smoke wreathed over him, Jackson lay on the floor and groaned his last. The bandit chief pointed his smoking gun at Seth. 'You got any problem, mister?'

'You rotten bastard!' Rita was struggling up from the couch. 'You didn't give him a chance.' She swung her handbag as a weapon. 'Poor Jack was my pal.'

'Go an' join him!' A rifle shot crashed out and Rita gasped with astonishment as the bullet skittled her flying back against the wall. Within seconds what spark of life there was in her eyes faded and she stared at them glassily unseeing.

When Espinosa turned to take a look and Ruth screamed with shock, Seth took his chance, pulling his Bowie. But as he raised it to hurl, a carbine butt thudded across the back of his neck and he hit the floorboards, poleaxed. *El*

*Borracho*, who had come in by the kitchen door, gave a deep-chested guffaw as he stood over him and smashed the carbine against the *gringo's* temple. He stepped over him, more interested in a sup of the tequila. He tipped up the bottle to his lips and glugged it down, heartily.

The Mexican with his rifle took his time reloading. 'She asked for it,' he said. The barkeep watched them, frozen like a startled rabbit.

'Yes, be warned, *querida*.' Espinosa stroked a finger down Ruth's cheek as she stared with horror at the blood oozing from Seth's head. 'Don' you go causing us no trouble. Come on, let's get out of here before the whole damn town comes looking.'

He jerked Ruth's head and led her out to the horses. 'Get on,' he ordered. 'Once we're down through the big canyon to the plain they'll never catch us.'

*El Borracho*, the tequila bottle in his fist, ran out to clamber on his mount.

'Meh-hee-co, here we come,' he roared and went galloping away after the others.

★   ★   ★

A bushy-bearded, gnarled face beneath a tam-o-shanter beamed down at him as Seth emerged from his blackout. The Scotsman dabbed at his temple with a damp cloth, staunching the blood. 'Ye're gonna have one heck of a headache, laddie. Can ye git up?'

'Yes.' Seth was helped to his feet. 'Quick, gimme your revolver, Dick.' He lurched towards the saloon door. 'I gotta go after 'em.'

He ran along the dusty street, his head suddenly spinning, sprawling full-length, but got groggily back on his feet and reached the smithy's. Star was already saddled and he tightened the cinch and scrambled on to his back, spurring him shooting away out of the barn door, and charging after the bandits.

Dick McGhee, with his trusty Hawken in his hands, watched him go. 'He's in an aw'mighty hurry.'

They had a long start on him, but maybe weren't expecting to be followed and the Arab stallion was built for speed. However, Seth let him settle into a steady lope to reserve his strength. It might be a long race.

He was helped by the fact that the Arkansas River at first began its descent through gentle timbered foothills to the plain. Seth stood in the stirrups, urging Star on, peering ahead. He had to catch up with them before the river reached the Grand Gorge. 'Go on, boy,' he yelled in the stallion's ear, putting him to a fast-drumming gallop. 'Go!'

Suddenly he heard the roar of the rapids as the river tumbled into the sheer-sided canyon, its pink granite walls in places a thousand feet high. No horse could follow through there. The trail would gradually veer away giving access to the plains.

'There they are!' he shouted, as he

saw them on the peak making their way along the precipitous cliffs. He whipped the stallion with the reins making him charge at breakneck speed through the rocky terrain. Maybe he could cut them off. It was worth a try.

Somehow the sure-footed, graceful horse negotiated the pitfalls and reached a pinnacle. Now they were only 400 yards away. Seth swung down from Star and pulled Christian Sharp's single-shot from the blanket roll. The three Mexicans were riding along the edge of the cliff; the girl, almost naked now as the wind whipped at her ragged dress, was hanging to her mustang as she was led along by Espinosa's noose.

The frontiersman knelt, jerked down the trigger guard, to expose the breech, fed a paper cartridge into it, snapped the guard up into place, shearing off the cartridge, exposing the powder to the capflash. They were a hundred yards away now, level with him. He squeezed the trigger, the shot cracked out and, almost simultaneously, the Mexican with the rifle threw up his hands and tumbled from his horse.

'What the devil!' Espinosa spun his mustang around. 'Where did that come from?'

With practised fingers Seth had already taken another cartridge from his pouch and fed it into the Sharps. He levered and sent another bullet whining past them, searing Espinosa's upper arm. The bandit pulled out his revolver, firing wildly, but at that range was ineffectual.

'*Hombre feo!*' he screamed. 'You dare to attack us?' He pulled the girl on her horse to the front of him. 'You ugly *gringo* pig. Now try it.'

'We'll kill her,' *El Borracho* roared, brandishing his Volcanic. 'If you shoot again, she goes.'

'See if you can stop me,' Seth hollered, getting to his feet, laying the Sharps aside and drawing McGhee's revolver. It was an ancient, inaccurate weapon. What chance had he against two expert gunmen? But he started leaping across the rocks towards them.

'Get off your horse!' Espinosa shouted at Ruth. He leaped from his own and dragged her down towards him. He caught tight hold of the rawhide noose and backed away towards the edge of the cliffs which at this point had dipped to about 200 feet in sheer height. He raised his revolver. 'Come on, shoot; I dare you.'

Seth leaped from rock to rock to face them. He needed to get to close range. He was looking into the deathly barrel holes of their weapons as they waited for him. How much closer dare he go?

Suddenly there was the clap of a rifle shot from half a mile away. A slug came whining and spinning through the air. It was fired by Dick McGhee, who had pounded along on his mustang and caught up with them. The old back-woodsman had carefully adjusted his sights, taken full account of wind strength and with breath-taking accuracy triggered the bullet's flight. It smashed through *El Borracho*'s chest just as he fired his Volcanic at Seth. The big giant went flying backwards, dead before he hit the ground.

Ruth took advantage of the surprise to gather her strength and jerk her elbow back to viciously jab into Espinosa's gut.

'You bitch!' he gasped, and kicked her backwards over the cliff, letting the rope go.

Seth heard her scream and fired, his first shot creasing Espinosa's side, his second cracking the bone of his thigh, and the third hitting him in the neck. He, too, slipped backwards, lost his footing and was hanging on desperately by his fingertips.

'Help me, *gringo*,' he pleaded, his eyes staring. 'Please.'

Seth hit him with the revolver butt, sending him flailing back to smash on to the rocks far below. He peered over the edge and saw the girl struggling in the maelstrom of raging water. Without hesitation he leaped out as far as he could and the wind seemed to surge through his stomach to his mouth as he dropped.

He hit the water and was swept on after her, almost drowned by the force of the snowmelt flood, but regained his senses, fighting to ride the crashing backwash, sliding over submerged rocks.

An increased roar warned of even greater danger ahead. The chasm narrowed into rambunctious rapids and certain death.

Seth was gasping for air, swallowing water. He went with the flow, swept onwards with the raging torrent, and saw her in front of him, the gleam of her pale body and golden hair, being tossed hither and thither like a cork. Suddenly a fallen tree was jutting out and, by some fortune of fate, she snatched out at its branches and hung on.

Seth swam with all his might towards her, grabbed her body and pulled her out on to the strip of bank. He lay gasping for breath stretched out on top of her lissom limbs. Ruth's eyes opened and she tightened her arms around him as she murmured, 'They said you'd gone back to your Indian wife.'

'No,' he smiled, kissing her. 'You're the only wife for me.'

'Where's Espinosa?' she asked.

'He's dead. They're all dead. You're safe now.' He raised himself up over her and grinned. 'Ain't it funny what you do to a man? All I want to do right now is make love to you.'

'You'll have to wait. We're being watched.'

Seth looked up from their shadowy depths to the crack of blue sky far above. The Scotsman had tied five lariats together and was lowering the end down. 'Quit that kissin',' he hollered, 'an' come on up. Ye'll have plenty of time for that the rest of ye're lives. Ye should see all the silver and gold up here I've found!'

We do hope that you have enjoyed reading this large print book.

Did you know that all of our titles are available for purchase?

We publish a wide range of high quality large print books including:
**Romances, Mysteries, Classics**
**General Fiction**
**Non Fiction and Westerns**

Special interest titles available in large print are:
**The Little Oxford Dictionary**
**Music Book, Song Book**
**Hymn Book, Service Book**

Also available from us courtesy of Oxford University Press:
**Young Readers' Dictionary**
**(large print edition)**
**Young Readers' Thesaurus**
**(large print edition)**

For further information or a free brochure, please contact us at:
**Ulverscroft Large Print Books Ltd.,**
**The Green, Bradgate Road, Anstey,**
**Leicester, LE7 7FU, England.**
**Tel:** (00 44) 0116 236 4325
**Fax:** (00 44) 0116 234 0205

When Hal Grant's father was bushwhacked in the street, it was the opening shot of a range war. Wealthy ranchers were determined to rid Lundon County of its sharecroppers and sodbusters eking out an existence in the marginal lands. Hal should have sided with his fellow ranchers, but he did not believe in mob law. He was caught in the middle — and no one was allowed to sit on the fence in a conflagration that was consuming a county . . .

# THEY CALLED HIM LIGHTNING

## Mark Falcon

A blow to the head had caused him memory loss and temporary blindness. Was he Mike Clancey, the name inscribed on the pocket watch he carried? And the beautiful woman's picture on the inside of the watch — was she his wife? He needed answers. Known as Lightning for his gun skills, riding Thunder, a black gelding, with fair play and talent he would bring a tyrant to justice — but it was a dangerous trail he must follow.